Mr. Crane, if you please

The First Novel in the Mr. Crane Series

Mr. Crane, if you please

Anthony Blossingham

Writers Club Press
San Jose   New York   Lincoln   Shanghai

Mr. Crane, if you please

All Rights Reserved © 2001 by Anthony Blossingham

No part of this book may be reproduced or transmitted in any form or by any means, graphic, electronic, or mechanical, including photocopying, recording, taping, or by any information storage retrieval system, without the permission in writing from the publisher.

Writers Club Press
an imprint of iUniverse.com, Inc.

For information address:
iUniverse.com, Inc.
5220 S 16th, Ste. 200
Lincoln, NE 68512
www.iuniverse.com

This Novel is a work of fiction. Names, characters, places, and incidents, either are products of the author's imagination or are used fictitiously. Any resemblance to actual events, locales or persons, living or dead, is entirely coincidental.

Cover Artwork by Melissa Atherton

ISBN: 0-595-00175-0

Printed in the United States of America

Dedication

This book is dedicated to everyone who offered me a smile, that was kind to a skinny kid with a great imagination. To my future wife, how I cannot wait to be with you. Though your name and face are not for me to know yet, the idea of you is always with me.

Foreword

The character of Mr. Crane was developed over 14 months, when I first thought of a merciless Hitman with a touch of honor. The short stories of Mr. Crane were done over an additional three months while spending the summer of 1999 in Arcadia, Michigan. The final writing of the novel was completed during the last three months of 1999, by using the previous short stories as a framework. It was pieced together one piece at a time, as most things are.

The secret I've found to my personal experience of writing a novel is to keep yourself entertained by the story. Forget your target audience, simply tell the story so that you enjoy and believe it. Also, remember that the first draft of anything is rough and lacking. Rewriting is the key. Don't be afraid to change your first draft. It is your right to let the work change and live during the writing process.

Finally, enjoy yourself. It's supposed to be fun, an obsession. If you aren't excited about writing on your novel, go outside or find someone to fall in love with. Do something other than get frustrated. Ernest Hemingway said a writer should stop when they reach a point in the story where they are sure they know what will happen next. He called it 'replenishing the inkwell.' I listened to that advice. Perhaps you will too.

Anthony Blossingham
Swartz Creek, Michigan
1/9/2000

Acknowledgments

I would like to thank Joe & Temma Simo, Nick "Pool Shark" Somero and all of the patrons from the Big Apple Bar and Grill in Arcadia. Thank you for allowing me to write in that dark corner, which was the inspiration for Mr. Crane's booth.

To the residents of Arcadia, thank you for sharing a beautiful shoreline and for showing me that the world still has villages that are as welcome as Eden.

To my mother Andrea, thank you for giving me confidence in my writing and my ability to just be me. I would not be the man I am today if it was not for you.

To my father Ward, thank you for teaching me that a man makes his own fun, heartache, and destiny.

To Melissa Atherton, whose talented artwork has turned a skinny writer into the man in the darkened booth. You have done the impossible; you have given a face to the mysterious Mr. Crane.

Editorial Method

My Editorial Method is not that complicated. First, I write down an outline for the book, the broad strokes so to speak. Then I attack the book, one section at a time. Once I've completed the sections as a first draft, I put them in order and fill in the cracks and I create segues. I then rewrite the book, starting from the first page until the entire book has been rewritten into a seamless piece. When I feel there is no more I can add to the text, I let someone very critical read it. I find someone who is good at finding mistakes and inconsistencies. I use their knit picking to my advantage. After I've corrected the errors, I send it back to them. Once they give it their seal of approval, I send it in to the publishers and I hold my breath. That is my Editorial Method.

Chapter 1

A Packed Duffel and Knapsack

The farmhouse had been covered in fresh rain the night before, dropping almost 3 inches. The smoke was coming out of the cobblestone chimney; the smell of sausage and the sound of a crackling fire were everywhere. The smells and sounds seemed to spill into the fields and the nearby woods.

Inside the house, Jacob George James sat and ate his breakfast. He had celebrated his high school graduation the night before, having a fun time before the rain fell. He was a lanky, skinny young man; though surprisingly strong in his shoulders. He had gotten so strong from working and growing up on that little farm in Bishop Springs, Minnesota. It was the faceless sort of town that did not make you want to stop and look around. It had a bank, a grocery store, and there was always talk of a hardware store being built, although it just amounted up to rumor.

Jacob was sick of that little farming community. He was leaving. Yet, instead of travel plans and adventures to be thought over, Jacob was distracted by the uneasiness that had enveloped the house.

He and his father, Mr. Doyle James, hadn't said a word that entire morning. Jacob's Mother, Emily, was standing her post at the kitchen stove, flipping the pancakes and browning the pork sausage. She had ground it that morning, then formed it into patties before Jacob woke up.

She had a pair of jeans and a flannel shirt on, with her hair put up in a do-rag. She put the finished pancakes and sausages onto separate plates, leaving them on the table for Jacob to replenish his now empty plate. Jacob forked a few patties and one more pancake, smothering all with large gobs of maple syrup. He spun the pancake triangle that he had cut out in the syrup, then he added a piece of sausage to the bite. He loved his mom's breakfast. He knew it would be something to miss when he was gone.

While drinking down his glass of cold milk, Jacob wished that his father would at least come in and eat at the same table as him. Emily had taken Doyle his breakfast out on the back porch, as he requested. She came in and just shook her head. She was ashamed of how her husband was acting but could do nothing about it.

Jacob could hear the clanking of his father's fork as it dropped onto his plate, then there was silence. Doyle poked his head into the kitchen and reached from the doorway into the silverware drawer. He leaned so far over, avoiding contact with the kitchen floor as if it were made of eternally hot lava. He first pulled out a spoon, then a salad fork, and finally a dinner fork. Instead of putting the spoon and the wrong fork back right then, he took them out on the porch. He would put them back after "he" was gone. "He," being Jacob.

"I'll be outside if you need me Emily." Doyle said through the screen-door. It was the first time Jacob had heard his father address his mother as Emily. He did it to exclude Jacob.

Doyle stepped down the molded concrete steps, nearly slipping on the bottom step. He gripped the railing and steadied himself. After a few choice words, he kicked the bottom step and hurt his big toe. Doyle limped out to the barn and began his day as if nothing out of the ordinary were occurring. To him, nothing was.

His early morning hours were kept busy with tending to his chores. When the pigs were fed, the cows were milked, and the fresh eggs were collected, Doyle moved onto the coops and then the fields. He grew mostly corn but Emily had a small garden that had everything from Tomatoes to Swiss Chard in it. He watered it to the point of drowning the plants. He just thought they could use a good soaking.

Making a living owning the farm was becoming next to impossible. Every day, surrounding farms were being foreclosed. Families that had owned land in that town for five generations were moving to the big city. Emily was now thinking about the hard times as she washed the dirtied breakfast dishes. She had her doubts as all farm wives do. She had to think positive though, she told herself. I have to look at it from the right angle is all.

Jacob did not agree. Nothing related to the farm seemed worth keeping. He would sooner sell the farm and move into town, sparing him and his family the embarrassment of being the last family to fold their tents.

Doyle understood that way of thinking and tried to agree with his son. It would have been easier to move to town before, but now all the other farmers that were holding out were looking to him for leadership. He thought about that whenever he had the twinge to sell. That morning, Doyle had more than a twinge. Keeping the farm was going to cost him his son.

Doyle and Emily were hard working people, having grown up on farms themselves. They were not the sort to go to church, but they had a pleasant way about them that told anyone in need that they would be happy to lend a hand.

Jacob was raised in a warm family, in that sleepy farming community. It was the closest thing to heaven for his parents, yet he wanted to leave. He thought of Bishop Springs as Purgatory; it was a place of indecision and limbo. He couldn't choose anything there because none of it mattered to him. His mother tried to make the farm work more interesting, but he would do his chores with the same monotonous movement. Doyle sensed this and told him to "stop this foolish behavior and learn to like the farm."

"It sounds like good advice, you'd be a fool not to take it," Jacob would often tell himself.

"Who are you talking to?" Doyle would ask with a look of surprise.

"Just thinking out loud," Jacob would say back.

He and his father had an unspoken competition going, each sure that the other was dead set in his opinions. He didn't hate the farm; he just wanted a change. Emily had told Doyle that very same thing that morning and it didn't make a difference in curbing Doyle's anger.

After Emily took a shower and prepared herself for the ride to the bus station, Jacob began to get his things together.

"Are you all packed?" She asked him.

"Yes ma'am," he replied.

"Got enough socks and underwear?" She asked as she looked into his packed duffel bag.

"Yes ma, all taken care of." He said with a tired voice.

"Good. Now here's a few dollars for the bus ride, in case you get hungry."

"Thanks ma." Jacob said to her smiling face.

"That's okay. You get your stuff together and meet me down at the car. I'm gonna go see if your father would like to join us."

"He won't come. He didn't even want to eat breakfast at the same table as me."

"He's hurting honey. He knows that you're not a farmer and that hurts him. That's not your fault, it's his. He just can't imagine you any other place but here."

Emily went down the creaky steps and turned right into the kitchen. She grabbed her jacket off the hook and slid it on as she went out the door. It wasn't warm for a day in May but it had a nice working outdoors temperature. It was as if an early autumn day had been transplanted five months ahead of time.

"Doyle? Doyle?" Emily called out to the barn then the coop. Nothing. "Doyle?"

"Yeah?" Doyle answered.

"You want to go with us to the station?" Doyle gave her a disgusted look.

"I think it would be good for you." She yelled out to him.

"Him leaving is the best thing for what I have." He yelled back.

"Have it your way." She replied.

"Thank you, I will." Doyle walked back into the field and continued spraying for bugs. The crop had just begun to break through the soil and he intended on seeing them safely through to harvest time. He pictured the harvest without the boy, all by himself, trying to operate the combine and the sorter. This made him even angrier and he walked deeper into the field, farther away from the house.

Emily went back into the house to collect Jacob and his things. There was only a duffel bag on the table so she picked it up by its strap and pulled it to the back door. She could hear Jacob walking around his room on the second level and decided to give him a moment of privacy as he gathered the last of his things.

He walked around his room and collected knickknacks that he would want to take with him. With a screwdriver and a freehand, he pried up a loose floorboard and pulled out a satchel of coins and a few paper bills. He counted it once, then twice. The third time counting it, he wrote the number down on a piece of scratch paper. The amount was enough for the bus ticket; a trip to a town that had no problem with inspiring young writers. He collected the money and put it into a cloth Royal Canadian satchel.

He sat on his bed, compressing the mattress with him and the weight of the knapsack. The room looked so small and it surprised him of how quickly he was able to pack up every worthwhile item in his room. He stood up and walked over to his window. Looking out, then down onto the car, he saw his mom carrying his duffel. He realized that he couldn't just stand there reminiscing anymore, so he turned from the soft light that filtered through his window and walked across the cold wood floor. Before walking through the door, he reached over to his desktop and grabbed a piece of paper. It was the crumpled bus schedule that he had carried everywhere with him and it fit easily into his shirt pocket. Looking back into his room, he casually put his jacket on and slung the knapsack onto his eager shoulder.

"All set?" Emily asked as she stood next to the car. She had already packed the duffel in the back of the beat up Chevy truck. Jacob took a deep breath of the air and it smelled clean and new.

"I'm set."

"Good, let's get moving." Emily jumped into the truck and started the engine. She turned the vents off and the radio on. Her left hand was occupied with readjusting the left side mirror while her right moved the rearview one. Jacob had to roll down his window to move the mirror on his side. He moved it in, and then he had to push it back out. Once those were set, she put the truck in "drive" and they were off like a heard of racing turtles.

"Have you talked with Jilly?"

"Last night. She said she'll have a bed waiting for me."

"You tell her thank you for me." She told him.

"Why? She's not doing you a favor?" Emily turned to look at him then said, "Just thank her for me. Christ. You and your father are going to give me a heartattack." She knew that putting Jacob in the same category as Doyle would put his smart remarks in their place.

"I can't believe how far Jilly has come since she left home."

"I know. That's what I want people to say about me."

"They will son, you just have to give it time. This too shall pass." Jacob thought about Jilly and how alike they were. She was a young girl who had left her father's farm at 16 and was a budding businesswoman by 20. She would often send Jacob letters inviting him over to stay, but always he couldn't go. There was harvesting to be done, or shingling to be repaired, or cows to be milked, or his mother wasn't well or they couldn't spare him, etc.

Although he always declined her offers to come stay, she kept sending him packages filled with magazines and goodies. She once sent him an old whiskey barrel that had a typewriter packed inside.

He was so grateful for the typewriter that the first thing he wrote with it was a 'thank you' letter to her. Then he wrote a short story about a farm-boy who runs away. Then came some poems, song lyrics, and the beginnings of a novel. Jacob had those writings with him, tucked in his knapsack, traveling with him to the bus station and all points afterward. He wished he could have brought the typewriter but it had been broken for a while and Doyle wouldn't fix it for him.

Jilly had phoned him the night before and double-checked the time of the arrival of his bus. It wouldn't be until 3 a.m. the following day because the bus would have to travel down through Wisconsin, Illinois, Indiana, then back north through Michigan.

Jacob thought, with the wind blowing through his open truck window, that he could easily find somewhere to work when he got to Arcadia. He figured that there would be tons of job openings for young men that were willing to work hard.

Emily occasionally glanced at Jacob, sometimes seeing him mouth words, knowing that he was imagining a conversation so she didn't call any attention to it. Maybe he was working on one of his stories? She considered silently. They continued to drive down the roads, pieces of gravel knocked and smacked the inner wheel wells. It had the distinct sound of trying to put wood chips in a blender.

Once they reached Nellie Lane, the dirt road turned into much quieter blacktop. Jacob sat up in his seat and scanned the street signs. The bus station was in the center of town, near the livery and grain elevator. They were getting close to the railroad tracks that ran right through town and everyone that lived in Bishop Springs gave lost motorists directions in relation to those tracks.

The buses would stop in Bishop Springs, once every three days, to pick up and drop off passengers and packages. Jacob loved to go into town, especially on the days the buses would arrive. It was great to see those silver bullet buses pull up in a convoy.

Jacob and Emily had arrived a few minutes early, just as she had planned. She was a punctual woman, almost to a fault. Jacob talked to her about the future, filled with writing projects, travel, and interesting people. She wanted to tell him to stay, but she didn't. She then wanted to go with him, but she couldn't. They sat there in the parking lane out in front of the station and talked.

Emily asked, "Will you call me when you get there?"

Jacob promised, and she let out a sigh of relief. They got out of the truck, Jacob tending to his duffel and knapsack, while his mom walked around to the front.

"You know what? I think I should do this on my own." She turned to him surprised by his comment; "You don't want me to wait with you?"

"I don't think you need to stand out here in the wind, on this cold platform."

Emily understood what her son was saying. She went up to his tall frame, and planted a kiss on his high-up cheek.

"Make yourself proud," she whispered, then hugged him.

"I will. I love you ma." Jacob was starting to cry, so he walked over to the concrete bench and began to wait.

He looked back over his shoulder a few times, seeing Emily walk slowly to the truck, apparently in no hurry to get back to the farm.

The anticipation of seeing the huge lake made him fidgety. He knew he had just a little longer to wait so he jumped up from the bench and quickly walked to the pop machines. His mother had driven away and he felt free to get up and explore the station. It was a temporary distraction before embarking on his trip. The duffel sat heavy on his shoulders, the knapsack in his right hand. He neared the ticket booth, seeing that there was a set of blinds in the window of the booth. He couldn't see if anyone was inside so he waited.

After he had set the duffel and knapsack down, a funny looking old man peered through the blinds then pulled the cord to raise them.

The man working behind the bus station window spoke, but the glass kept Jacob from hearing it clearly. The man saw that Jacob was having trouble understanding him, so he lowered his mouth to the money exchange slot and asked, "Bus to Arcadia?"

"Yes sir." Jacob replied.

"That'll be $70.00 please." He put the money into the slot; having to put his hand in with it, trying to make sure it wouldn't get stuck.

"There you are son, now it'll be ready to go in a few minutes. You may want to use the facilities. It's a long ride."

"Thanks for the advice." Jacob picked up the ticket and nodded towards him. He tucked it into his jacket and let his eyes adjust to the humming lights of the station.

"Can I put these somewhere?" He asked the old man about his bags.

"Sure, right here." The old man pointed down to a luggage bin. Jacob checked out the platform he was on and didn't see anyone else. He set the knapsack in first then the duffel. He was betting that the duffel would be too heavy for someone to run away with.

Now much lighter, Jacob cocked his head around, spying a bathroom door but then found out it was a ladies' room. He walked to the other side of the cement platform, expecting a men's restroom. He found it, but the door handle was missing and there was police tape across the door.

"You can use the ladies' room, just knock before you go in," said the old attendant, having come out from the warm office and onto the platform to load bags.

"Can I get your bags for you young man?" He asked as a little bit of snot gathered at the tip of his old nose.

"No, that's all right. I'll get them myself." Jacob replied.

"You got it. Short trip?" He asked.

"Not likely."

"Oh I see. Don't you worry boy, there's a big world out there." The old man's bony fingers pointing out over the trees.

"There's plenty of room for everyone to do some good living." Jacob hoped he was right.

It was odd for Jacob to hear someone so optimistic about his future, like he thought a father should be. Maybe this is as far as he had to go, finding a father at the bus station.

After he used the restroom, he returned to the luggage bin and retrieved his things. He tugged at the strap of his duffel and allowed the knapsack to lean against his thin leg. He waited patiently until he was given permission to board. He nervously climbed into the warm bus, with its gray upholstery, perfect for hiding stains. Jacob chose a seat near a window, thinking he had lucked out. He honestly didn't know what made a seat lucky. This was the first time he had been on a bus.

Everyone else arrived at the time of departure, slowly loading up their loved ones and over packed bags. Jacob just sat there watching them all; confident that someday he would join their ranks. He would stand tall, with a smile to show for all the fame and adventure that he'd be a part of.

He had spent nearly all of his money just getting the ticket to Arcadia. An hour into the trip, the bus broke its rear axle, so the passengers were off loaded and asked to wait in a nearby diner. Jacob carried his heavy duffel and knapsack across the gravel lot and into the little truckstop dive. He chose a booth near the door and was handed a menu by a pink outfit-wearing waitress. She had her red hair up into a ball of curls. The receipt pad and pencil that she carried with her were in a front pouch and she was doing her best to be polite.

"What'll you have?" She asked. Jacob looked up to her and saw the worried look that grew with every second. She was seeing the stranded passengers walk across the lot and into her diner. This is gonna suck, she thought to herself.

"I'll take an orange juice and um…" Jacob poked through the coins in his right hand, not wanting to break his twenty dollar bill so early in the trip, "I'll just have the juice." She snatched the menu from him and called back to the cook, telling him to get ready for a busy afternoon. He grumbled something and disappeared back into the walk-in freezer.

Jacob sat in the window side booth, staring out at the bus. There was no sign of a mechanic or wrecker coming to fix it. The driver came in after everyone else was safely in the diner. Jacob asked him, "How long do you think it'll be?"

"I've got no idea kid. Just have something to eat and wait like the rest of us." Jacob took his jacket off since he would be staying for a while. The juice was dropped off at his table and he barely had time to say 'thank you' before the waitress tore off to handle another order.

He sipped the juice slowly, tasting the pulp stick to the inner wall of his mouth. The other passengers were eating lunches: sandwiches with French fries, salads, soups, and every kind of pie in existence. Though Jacob wished he could eat like them, he was content with his juice. It was cold, not too pulpy, and it wasn't bitter. He smacked his lips after the fourth gulp, seeing that the glass would be empty after the next gulp. Keep your money in your pocket; it's going to be a long trip he reminded himself. I don't need steaks or pie. I'm fine with this juice. I'll just sit here and wait. That's what I'll do. God I wish I had eaten more breakfast.

The bus driver finished his lunch and stood to make an announcement, "Folks, I need you all to get your things and come with me out to our new bus. My bosses have just called," he held up his cell-phone, " and they're sending a backup ride. So please make sure you have everything." Everyone paid their bill, and quickly marched out into the slightly warmer air. Jacob would have benefited from hearing that message, but he was in the restroom going poop. By the time he had read the commentary section of the Williamsburg Herald, he came out to his booth to find all the others gone. He rushed to the window and stood there confused. The bus was still there, still broken, but where was everyone?

"Excuse me, where did everyone go?" He asked the waitress.

"They left about ten minutes ago."

"What?"

"I said ten minutes ago. They left. As in no longer here." She turned her back to Jacob and went back to the register to tally up the mound of receipts.

"What am I going to do? What the hell, am I, going to do?" He asked himself with segmented breaths.

"Hey kid. You one of them bus people?" A dirty, slovenly dressed old woman asked.

"Yes ma'am. Or at least I was."

"Where you heading?" Jacob was dreading this; he could feel a proposition coming on. He swallowed the knot is his throat and answered, "Arcadia, Michigan." The woman reared back in a mix of surprise and disgust.

"You can just take the Ferryboat over. Hell, it'll save you a day's trip."

"Where is this Ferryboat?" She pointed out the window with a vague finger. "Yes I know it's out there. Could you be more specific?" She stood up and pointed to the big red sign in the diner's parking lot that read 'Ferryboat Service-2 miles.' Jacob turned and thanked her with his duffel and knapsack hanging heavily.

The walk to the Ferryboat dock wasn't very exciting, with Jacob complaining about the broken down bus and being left behind. The gnats and the flies listened to him as they dive-bombed his sweaty forehead, reaching for a sweet drop. He swung the light knapsack at them and occasionally got a buckle or a zipper in the face. He gave up on killing them so he tried out running them. The dust from the dirt road was laying low and didn't kick up when he ran from the bugs. He made it 15 yards before stopping, so sure of outrunning the crap jumpers, as his father called them.

He could see the bend in the road that led to a body of water down the road. He walked for half the way but then he began to worry about missing the next scheduled boat, so he struggled to run the rest of the way.

The depot of the Ferryboat had a turnstile gate that could only be passed if you put a token in. The tokens cost $10.00, and Jacob still didn't want to break his twenty. He told the gatesman that he was with a party of people who had pre-paid. The man looked at Jacob and then a list of people, then waved him through the turnstile.

Jacob made a point of disappearing once onboard. He didn't want that gatesman to check out his story any further and make him get off. Instead of joining the paying riders in the 'Hot Chocolate Lounge' or so the sign said, he went up top to the open-air deck.

The sun shined through the thinnest of clouds but it was quickly covered by the dark boomers that came off the lake. He had grabbed a travel itinerary about the boat ride. It said that the trip began in Williamsburg, where he was, and then it headed directly east over to Ludington. It would only take 4 hours compared to the 15 spent riding down and around the lake on a bus.

He put the brochure away and made himself as comfortable as possible. He kept his back to the railing and sat on the deck. He watched the stairwell until they had left the dock and were well out into the lake.

Every once in a while, people would go up to look around then they'd go back down to the cafe. Jacob still had his twenty and some loose change after paying for his delicious lunch time juice. He was in the middle of getting his money out to recount it but he feared losing it to the wind.

Since he had never been on a boat or a body of water that size, he felt uneasy. He didn't want to call it fear because that scared him too much. Instead he called it excitement and that kept the irrational thoughts about the boat sinking, from taking over. He buttoned up his jacket and wished that it would start feeling like May.

He tucked his face down into his jacket and tried to fall asleep. The wind was just too strong and like everyone else, he went down to the cafe.

The hot chocolate was free, because it was simply hot water with brownish bubbles of sugar floating in it. Jacob had two. Then he took a pee and had another. He found a bench in the back, sure that no one else wanted to sit there, and after he removed his jacket, he laid his things down under the bench and slept. He didn't dream about anyone in particular, he just floated in and out of light slumber.

The cabin usher woke him when they were thirty minutes out from shore. Jacob grabbed his duffel and his jacket and slowly made his way up to the top deck again. This time, there was land in front of him and lake behind. This pleased him tremendously. He made sure his jacket was zipped up all the way. The collar covered his neck very well and so he stayed there, leaning against the railing, shouting "so long Minnesota, here I come Arcadia!" until the boat was docked.

On shore, groups of people were standing together to greet family members who were returning home or coming over for a visit. No one was waiting for Jacob. He hadn't called Jilly about missing the bus and he really didn't want to break that twenty. Collect calls were just in case of an emergency so he just waited his turn in the debarking line. He stepped down the gangplank and felt better that he was on land again.

There was a definite smell of fish when he walked down the dock and onto dry land. His legs felt like jelly, since they were still readjusting to phantom waves. He walked up the concrete slab sidewalk and onto the main drag. There was a bus stop but it was a metropolitan route, so he needed to find some other way to Arcadia or at least to Manistee. Manistee was north of Ludington and south of Arcadia. He'd shoot for Arcadia but most likely, he'd have to settle for Manistee. Settle he reluctantly did.

He ended up hitching a ride to Manistee with a married couple that worked as truck drivers. They had a rig with a big bed in the back, so if she got sleepy, he'd take over and vice versa. They had pictures of their dogs; two beagle pups with sad droopy eyes. The wife told Jacob that the dogs were happy staying at her sister's place, which was a dairy farm. Nevertheless, Jacob seriously doubted the happiness of staying on a farm.

They took him as far as Moo-Mooville. The weather was finally usual for May, with the sun brightly shining. He had forgotten to pack shorts and was now sweating like you wouldn't believe. He didn't understand why it was so temperate in Michigan while Minnesota had an overcast fixation when it came to early summer weather.

He walked down the right shoulder of the highway and kept his eyes fixed on the ground in front of him. There was a weird fella who wanted to give him a ride, but Jacob said it was a good day for walking. He started screaming and shouting, "you damned bastard, I'll kill you!" Jacob pulled out the Swiss army knife he got from cub scouts and pulled the blade just in case. The strange man stopped the car and just leaned over from the driver side seat, calming down and wiping the anger from his wrinkled face, "come on kid, I've got some candy."

Jacob bolted. Running faster than he'd ever thought possible; at least for those scrawny legs. He had all he could stand from that little man in the green Dodge Dart. The creepy old guy chased after him in his car until a state trooper drove by. The creep drove past Jacob as he ran the best as he could with his duffel and knapsack. Jacob looked over to the road and saw the smile on the old man's face. Jacob twisted his head to look forward and focused on continuing his run. He made it until the Dart was out of sight and he slowed down. Keep walking, he told his tired legs, keeping his eyes peeled for the old creep or someone like him. Jacob trudged past countless mile markers and finally stopped, out of breath and scared as hell.

Chapter 2

▼

The Arcadian Streets

That freaky episode with the old creep had drained his energy more than being abandoned at the Diner had. It made him think more than twice about hitching.

Examining the road ahead, he saw that the final leg of his trip to Arcadia would be all-uphill. He didn't have the muscles or the time to try to walk it. Besides, it was going to get dark around 8 p.m. and that meant he had nearly three hours of daylight.

He convinced himself he'd be all right, just as he accepted a ride from a group of migrant workers stuffed in the back bed of a beat-to-hell Ford Pickup truck.

Jacob held his hands out to a seven-year-old little boy and asked him "what do you prefer" in Spanish. He showed the boy a candy bar in one hand and a couple pieces of hard candy in the other. Jacob had been saving the sweets for when he got too hungry to wait for an Arcadian dinner, but he knew that the boy would appreciate it more. The little boy, with dark brown eyes and cheerful face, pointed to the chocolate bar and shouted, "gracias!"

Jacob smiled back at the group of ranch hands and fruit pickers, seeing such familiar manners and kindness. Growing up on the farm had exposed Jacob to other cultures and languages.

"De nada, El Nino." Jacob replied to the boy with half the chocolate already eaten. The hot sun had melted it in its aluminum foil, so the boy scooped it up with his little fingers. Jacob could see he enjoyed it more that way. The father of the little boy nodded his head in a gesture of saying 'thank you' which Jacob happily returned.

The migrant workers that his father employed never liked being around him. They used to say to each other, "He has bad eyes." Jacob would hear this but he wouldn't say a thing. He didn't know what to say to them. Maybe they were referring to his temper, which sometimes got a little out of control, but never serious. Maybe it was their way of leveling the playing field. He had it easier than they did, so they might as well get a free kick.

The entire group found the trip sunny and pleasant. The others were used to the sweltering sunshine, whereas Jacob was without a hat or a chance for shade. He fanned his tanning face, though he was no longer sweating. The elder men laughed about his situation, but Jacob didn't mind. Jacob found out that it wasn't how weak he was to the heat that made them chuckle, it was the rest of the melted candybar which Jacob was sitting in. He looked over to the boy who had a chocolate smear across his mouth, the boy looked back. His eyes were so serious, like he expected Jacob to explode. Jacob kept a firm expression, just long enough to make eye contact with the elders, then he erupted in laughter.

The old women patted their chests and the men wiped their foreheads; for the first time, they were sweating. They had a good laugh about that melted candybar, letting it distract them from their windburns. Jacob asked the leader of the families to wake him when they got there, though he didn't expect to get a wink of sleep. He was too excited, and the constant bumps and noises didn't make for much of a quiet nap. It had been four hours since he had left home. His mother would eventually find the note he left her. It was hidden in her wicker laundry basket and it began with, 'I hope you understand. I want a life that can't be had on the farm. I know you understand ma, please help dad to.'

They went without supper as they noticed the sun finally going down. The families started pulling out blankets for the children and themselves. Jacob followed their lead; he put on another shirt and rezipped his jacket. He sat there shivering from the sudden cool-off, so used to that damned sun. Someone in the group started singing a bedtime song. Jacob thought it was a spiritual, because everyone clapped lightly and sang in unison. He just acted as if he knew the words, his Spanish unable to keep up with their proficient serenade.

It wasn't until 8:34 p.m. that they arrived. The comfortable nighttime welcomed them into town with the smells and sights that were strictly Arcadia. Jacob could hear his stomach growling, so he bid his new friends a safe journey and hopped out of the truck. He dragged his duffel off then he slid the knapsack onto his sore right shoulder.

From all the running, carrying and sitting in unpleasant situations, his body was ready for a break. He gazed down M-22, seeing the lights from the street corners brightening up sections of the black asphalt road. The lines running down the center were old and barely visible. Jacob reminded himself to stay on the mostly lit side to avoid any more creepy people.

It was only a three-minute walk into town from where the truck had dropped him off. He couldn't believe it; he was taking his first stroll in Arcadia. Lake Street was on his right as he went past a large white building. It had a painted sign on the wall, advertising that the business inside made their own ice cream. Jacob still didn't want to break that twenty so he sat on the park benches outside, breathing in the aroma of freshly baked pizzas. He could almost taste the pepperoni and sauce. He wanted to buy a slice; he still hadn't eaten since breakfast.

Just down the road, lit up by blinking lights and a yellow bug zapper was a restaurant. It looked very familiar. It looked like a restaurant in

Bishop Springs, which had been built on a piece of god-awful land in the middle of town. He shook off the Minnesota memories and realized that he was walking the turn of the century streets of Arcadia, looking for a bite to eat and directions to his cousin's house. He stuffed his jacket into his duffel with nervous hands that were being fed with shaky satisfaction over finally being there in Arcadia.

Since nothing else looked open, he gave Papa's Café a shot. He set the duffel and knapsack down under his table and then wiped his forehead with the paper napkin in front of him. The service in this little dive was almost as bad as the food. He waited and waited. Then he waited some more. Twenty minutes went by before he was given a menu. He had been the only customer in there the whole time!

He deflected the menu from the waitress's hand and just told her a cup of hot coffee was all he wanted. She made a slick comment as she walked over to the coffee machine. Jacob pretended not to hear. When she set the cup on the table, he put his finger in the center of it. It was ice cold.

"Oh Waitress!" He hollered over to her. She raised her eyebrows as if to ask, ' what do you want now?'

"This coffee is ice cold. I asked for hot coffee."

"So?"

"Nevermind. I'll never come in here again."

"Ouuuuu." She sarcastically replied.

"Ouuuuu indeed," Jacob muttered back to himself.

He thumbed through the money in his tired hands, counting out the bill. Jacob gave the unhelpful waitress, Tish Whiner, the fifty cents. He looked at the ignorant young woman and hoped that they'd never cross paths. She wouldn't remember him; he just had one of those easily forgotten faces, a blessing to someone who had spent a lifetime in a sawdust spotlight.

Chapter 3

Worker Wanted

Jacob felt an annoying feeling of dread; he was getting scared of the night ahead with nowhere to sleep if he couldn't find Jilly's place.

There was a distant booming; a cool breeze blew in from the lake. Though it was too dark to see it, he knew the lake was there. His tired fingers waited patiently for what he knew could only be rain. Jacob stood there, in that unfamiliar street, amidst houses and shops he'd never been to, and he let the rain wash away all the traces of the farm. Letting it baptize him as it soaked his clothes and the outer coverings of the bags he had brought with him.

He could see an old-style phone booth back near the corner General Store, so he walked over to use it.

Once inside, he put a slippery quarter into the slot. His fingers were cold and damp from the now falling rain. This had caused them to stick to the fabric in his jeans pockets, making it difficult for him to retrieve his money.

First he called his cousin's number, but he got a disconnected line message. He tried the number again, but again, the phone beeped disconnected. He even called the operator who was more than happy to tell him the number was no longer in service.

Eventually, after talking to the operator for what seemed like forever, she gave Jacob his cousin's home address. Jacob stood in the booth, out of the pouring rain, without a clue as to where his cousin's house was. He put the receiver back on the latch and made his way into the General Store. He tracked in some mud and stood there in front of the register, dripping wet.

"Towels are in aisle three," the checkout girl pointed out.

"No, I need to find out where this address is," Jacob said.

"Well," she looked down at the piece of paper in Jacob's shivering hands; "this place is one block over."

"Which way?" He asked in agitation.

"That way." She pointed towards the back of the store.

"Thanks." He ran off; mud, water, and cold. It didn't matter to him.

He ran to the back of the store, out through a squeaky screen door and then went across a vacant lot. He came to a fence that hadn't been repaired in years. He crawled under the wire and his bag got caught.

"Damn thing! Come on."

"Who's there?" A young woman's voice yelled out.

"Come on! Come on!" Jacob jostled the bag, frantic that he didn't recognize the voice.

"Get him boy." The voice said to its dog.

"For Christ-sake! Come on!" Jacob pulled with one strong tug, ripping the duffel open and throwing him down on top of his knapsack. His wet, scared face was met by the growls of a miniature Yorkie.

"Jacob? Is that you?" The voice now sounding familiar, the face behind the flashlight still unseen.

"Yeah, Jilly?"

"Oh god! How are you?" She asked as he was helped up. They collected the pieces of clothes that had fallen onto the muddy ground in Jilly's backyard.

"Good. I wanted to call but your number…"

"I know, I got a little behind in my bills," she shrugged, "next week it might be the lights."

"What are you doing here so early? You weren't supposed to get here until early tomorrow morning."

"I had to take the Ferryboat over. It's a long story. I'll tell you about it later. Can we go inside and get dry?"

"Sure, sorry about Mr. Weiser."

"You named you're dog Mr. Weiser?"

"Yep." She said proudly, taking Jacob's knapsack off his shoulder and into the back of the house. He was dragging the duffel as "Mr. Weiser" tugged on the strap.

"Why would you call a dog that?"

"It seemed like a good idea at the time." Jacob snickered at this.

"Come on in, we've got a lot to catch up on." They walked through the back door of the big farmhouse, stopping in the mudroom so Jacob could take off his shoes and filthy clothes. As he did that, Jilly went upstairs and retrieved some of her ex-boyfriends' clothes. They didn't fit Jacob, who was too thin and lanky, but they would have to do.

She readied the bathroom for him, showing where the towels and the soap were. She explained that the shower didn't work right so he'd have to take a bath. He acted like it didn't bother him, but in truth, Jacob hadn't taken a sit down bath in years. He was just too tall for tubs and this made cleaning those hard to reach places a near impossibility. He stripped down and took a seat in the empty tub. It needed a good scrubbing but the water flowed out clear and warm. He had expected to see the water run out dark brown, as if the toilet and tub were connected.

He was pleasantly surprised. With his legs dangling over the sides, he washed everything. Standing up was a trick since there was no skid mat on the bottom. He lurched forward then overcompensated and ended up against the back wall. Jilly heard the thump and came running. He could hear her leaning against the door, listening for some sign of Jacob.

"I'm all right. Just slipped a bit."

"Just be careful." She advised.

"No shit." He said under his breath.

After drying off, he stood in front of the fogged over mirror and couldn't see his reflection. Had he been home, he would have wiped it clear with the palm of his hand. There he didn't care about making streaks. Now that he was in Jilly's home, he left it covered. He just wanted something to eat and then to go to bed. Nevertheless, he knew he owed Jilly a long talk, so he put on a pair of boxers, then a T-shirt with sweatpants. He opened the door and let the mist escape out into the dining room. It was a big house, with large rooms and high ceilings.

"You need some socks on, there's tacks still in the floor." Jilly told him. The carpet had been ripped up and she was making do with the bare plywood floors. It didn't bother her that there were tiny nails sticking up all over. She just walked with him around the house and gave him the tour. Jacob thanked her for letting him stay with her. Then he thanked her for his mother Emily. After all, he promised to.

She was thrilled at the idea of having a roommate. Jacob just wanted some food. She told him to take a seat at the kitchen table, where she ate all of her meals, and went into the motions of making him a home-cooked dinner. She had chicken and potatoes, a small bundle of asparagus that she roasted on the griddle, and a bottle of cheap, but good, white wine. Once it was on the table Jacob dug in. He ate three chicken breasts, two helpings of asparagus, and one whole glass of wine. About the wine, Jacob wasn't much of a drinker, so one whole glass was an accomplishment. Jilly asked again about the trip, so he laid it out for her in melodramatic words. Instead of one creepy old man, it had been four tough looking bikers who were ready to rumble. She knew he was embellishing but it didn't make the story any less entertaining.

At the end of his story, he told her goodnight and walked over to the makeshift bed that had been laid out on the dining room floor. Jilly offered the room at the top of the stairs, the landing, but the bats and mice that Jacob found up there were too much to handle on just one glass of wine.

"Good night cousin." Jilly said to Jacob as he pulled the unfamiliar covers to his chin. He was tired and didn't want to think anymore about home. He didn't like sleeping in other people's houses, he felt like an obstacle to them. It seemed like he was interfering with the natural flow of their day.

"Shut up Jacob," he whispered to himself, "go to sleep. Close your eyes. Stop thinking. It's easy to do, just sleep." His eyelids were no match for that sort of persuasion, closing slowly with heavy certainty.

Jilly was in the kitchen washing up the dinner plates when her cellphone began to ring. It was Aunt Emily calling to make sure she was there for Jacob's arrival. She didn't know that he had already arrived. Jilly told her that he was sleeping right now but she could go and wake him. Emily said, "no that's okay. I'll just call tomorrow or have him call me collect."

"Okay Auntie."

"Night honey."

Jilly went back to the dishes and was startled by Jacob who was standing right beside her.

"Sorry. I walk kind of quiet."

"I'll say. That was your mommy." She was kidding with him.

"My mommy huh? Is she pissed at me for not calling?"

"Nah, you know you're ma."

"How about my dad, did you talk to him?"

"No, though I could hear him snoring in the background." Jacob grinned.

"I'm going back to bed. You can leave those dishes and I'll get them in the morning."

"Really?"

"Yeah. Men can do dishes too."

"All right then. I'm off to bed too."

"Night, again."

"Good night Jacob." They went to their beds and slept effortlessly.

The next morning went by fast since they both slept in until noon. That was okay for Jacob since he had no job to get to, but Jilly had to be at the Angel Store by One o'clock. She was ripping and tearing through the house, looking for one shoe then another, then a blouse and skirt. She jumped over Jacob's floor bed and marched into the bathroom to "put on my face," as she said it.

Jacob lay there in the warm covers until she was close to leaving for work. He got dressed in his hand-me down clothes and went out back to see what the yard looked like in the daytime. It was much bigger than he thought, with large spans of lawn and a fenced in garden. There was a plastic owl perched on top of a corner post, which stood guard against birds and any one that was afraid of plastic owls.

"Watch some TV or read or…. Whatever!' She yelled back to him as she went out the back door and jogged around to the corner, not yet late to her job. Jacob rubbed his face with his clammy hands and scratched the tip of his nose. He could feel the tenderness of a pimple so he stopped scratching. He didn't want to make it any redder.

Jilly had used her cell-phone with unfortunate regularity, and it was with that phone that Jacob called home to let his mother know that he had arrived the night before. His mom got on the line and she was trying to keep her composure, all the while Doyle was yelling about him not being meant for living in the city. Emily clenched the receiver and it was then that she whispered to him, in the strictest confidence, that he was right about leaving home.

She could hear his nervous voice, calming down then suddenly getting upset. He told her that he had plenty of money, but that was not what concerned her. It was the sound of his scared voice that made her want to bring him home so that he could feel safe again. However, she knew that wouldn't be for the best. She made him promise not to come home until the fear had gone away. She listened as a few tears fell on the receiver and then his nose began to stuff up. She let Doyle have the phone and through the muffled hand over his end of the line Jacob heard, "that son-of-a-bitch...we won't give him nothing. You hear me!" Leave it to Doyle to end a conversation on a high point. Jacob didn't have to say good-bye; Emily's usually quiet voice was heard arguing with her husband. Then there was nothing. A few seconds later, a blurred ringing of static filled the phone.

Jacob held onto the phone, hoping that somehow he'd have the money to make the trip work. He feared that he'd lose the nerve and go back home.

He set it down on the counter and went into the back washroom. He found that Jilly had hung his jacket up over the laundry tub, wanting to give it a head start in drying.

As he rang out his still-soaked clothes from the day before, he was glad he had made the trip. He couldn't see spending his life staring out from that Minnesota farmhouse wondering "what if."

He walked a little slower, breathed a little deeper. Jacob played the part of a lost soul to perfection. He was getting to know Jilly's house, where every little piece of cookery was kept, how she folded her clean towels in the hallway closet, etc.

He spent that first day inside, cleaning, washing, and cooking. Anything to feel useful. There wasn't much to clean; it was just busy work. Jilly came back home at five o'clock and Jacob had dinner on the table. There was a soft scent of lilac and Jilly could see the dryer sheets in the trash basket. She knew the laundry was also done.

"Let's eat," said Jacob, wearing one of her aprons.

"I thought it would be nice for you to meet one of my co-workers."

"Oh."

"Is there enough? Cause if there isn't it's no problem."

"No, are you kidding. With the way my ma taught me to cook? There'll be leftovers for weeks."

"Cool, I'll tell her to come right over."

Not even a minute went by before Jilly's co-worker/ friend was there.

"Hi, I'm Wendy. You must be Jacob."

"Must be." Jacob said shyly.

"Let's eat then…" Jilly interrupted.

"Yes, lets." Jilly told stories about Jacob and their growing up together. She told the story about Jacob and his prize calf, how it had won the blue ribbon and then ran away.

"Old Herb stayed around just long enough for me to win. I trained him well." They all laughed. Wendy Gibson was a pretty girl, who hadn't been raised on a farm like her dinner companions. She had grown up in Arcadia and co-owned the Angel Store. She had black hair and cute freckles on the bridge of her nose. She had a bit of a tomboy quality that made Jacob comfortable. All the girls that he'd known back home had that toughness. He was beginning to have the warm, dizzy sensation of a crush. That's when she said that she had a boyfriend. He was some big time writer for the local newspapers. She said it was difficult to break into that area's writing community. Jacob didn't want to hear that. He collectively quit listening once she said, " have a boyfriend."

It was getting to be around dusk and they said goodbye to Wendy, as the strong light of day became dark and soft. She was going back to the store to wait for her boyfriend to pick her up. Jacob shut the door once Jilly was done talking to Wendy. She went to the bathroom then came out and said, "I'm sorry about that. It's not fair to show you a great girl like that, then tell you she's taken."

"It doesn't surprise me. Most great girls are." They both agreed.

"You wanna go for a night walk?" She was putting her jacket on and shaking his out. "It's dry." She held it towards him.

"Sure. Show me around this busy metropolis." She led him out the front door and they walked down to Fourth Street. After making a left, they turned right on Lake Street and strolled past the Post Office and a Hair Salon.

Two identical looking collies barked at everyone and everything that passed by. Jacob waved at their owner, who was in the process of getting them back inside the house. They peered into the large windows of the museum, seeing a canoe, fishing poles and other old oddities. Right next to the museum was a classic car showroom. There were shiny European sports cars, convertible for sunny days and getting the ladies. Jacob wanted to know who owned them, Jilly didn't know.

She knew he was homesick, that he had never been off the farm. She told him the story about the Bigfoot sighting old Mrs. Macdonald claimed to experience. They both had a good laugh. That's why Jilly was so scared when Jacob had arrived, she had let herself think, for the briefest moment, that he was the Sasquatch.

They walked side by side, she on the sidewalk, he in the street. Jacob stumbled over the broken concrete and the tiny puddles that had formed from the last nights' downpour. Once they had thoroughly explored the downtown area, they went down to the turn-around. That was the parking lot to the Arcadia Beach, where the townspeople and tourists would go on hot summer days. Camp Arcadia, which was a religion based campground and resort, owned the land directly to the right of the Arcadia Beach. There were groups of staffers from the camp, boys and girls that were Jacob's age. The girls might have seen him, though the dark shadows cast from the turn-around's streetlight covered up whether or not they were checking him out. He was too poor to think so; Jilly pulled his arm in order to snap him out of his staring. He blushed as she walked him back toward downtown. They talked about the town and some of the things that Jacob would have to know. Mostly it boiled down to directions to the Angel Store, the Post Office, and the Big Apple Bar. Jilly sometimes went there with her friends after work. He wasn't legal to drink booze but he could just go to hang out and listen to the old jukebox.

After finding their way through Arcadia's quiet streets, they arrived at the doorway of the smoky little bar. The two cousins could hear music inside.

Jacob nearly died from shock, since right in the front window was a "worker wanted" sign. Jilly had brought him there for a reason.

"You're perfect for this job. You'll get to meet new and interesting people." She pointed out his messy hair, causing him to comb the strands back with his fingers as he stood in the middle of the sidewalk. Jilly wished him luck and asked if he needed her to wait. He said no, that he remembered the way to her house. She corrected him and told him that it was "their" house.

They said good-bye for the moment and Jacob began to get his courage up. He had to be civilized and there was no better place to show his middle-class upbringing than that blue-collar bar.

He took off his jacket as he stepped into the bar. The ceiling fans were turning slowly, the wind swept windows covered on the outside with large spots of dust. The whirling sounds from the fans were hypnotic, making him drowsy as he took his seat on the barstool. There were three other people in the place, not counting the old bartender.

"Whatcha have Mack?" The bartender asked.

"A job." Jacob replied.

"You some kinda smart-ass or something?" The gray haired man asked.

"No sir, just in need of some work…" He managed to say. The bartender looked at Jacob's face with his tired eyes, and knew he was telling the truth.

"A job it is. Oh by the way, I'm Frank Simona. You can call me Frank or Mr. Simona. Never sir." He leaned down to get an apron under the bar counter.

"Okay…Frank." He showed Jacob around the bar. The young man admired the architecture, making that little bar feel familiar. Frank occasionally looked back and wondered what he'd gotten himself into by hiring him.

Chapter 4

Kinda like Black Olives

He took Jacob to the side door and turned him around. They were facing into the main room, with the bar to their left, tables, and booths aligning the far wall all the way to the right. The booths had low hanging lamps to light up the dark spots. Oddly, there was one booth situated to the far right and it had no light over it.

"You want me to go check the bulb?" Jacob asked.

"No!" The old man answered, scaring the hell out of him.

"Why not?" Jacob said. The old man just looked at him and said to forget that booth. Jacob needed the job and did not want to piss him off, so he did as he was told.

They walked into the office that was tucked safely away in the back of the bar. He showed Jacob the collection envelopes and the safe. Then he showed Jacob a big knife. It was explained to him that the money goes into the envelopes, the envelopes go into the safe; and if Jacob stole any of the money, the butcher knife would go into him.

Jacob nodded, showing the old man he understood. They left the office and Frank stopped with his keys and locked the heavy metal door.

"You've got some serious doors here. Why?"

"Cause there's a lot of serious people that would love to get in there." Jacob laughed, Frank didn't.

Jacob was handed a broom and dustpan, and was told to sweep up the main room, since there were only a few people drinking that night, being Wednesday and all. Jacob emptied the dustpan and was washing his hands when that empty booth, in the far right corner, caught his eye. He looked over to the empty seating, finding the missing lightbulb wasn't replaced as Frank said he would. Jacob figured he'd gotten busy and so he tried to reach in, stretching to put a new bulb in, but a velvet rope guarded the lone booth. He looked around for Frank but he was back in the office.

"Here Frank, I'll change that bulb for you." He said to the back office, so sure Frank would appreciate the help. Frank tore through the office door and got between the darkened booth and Jacob.

"What's the matter? I'm just gonna…"

"Enough. You want this job? Do ya?" Frank said as he grabbed his shoulders and stared through him.

"Yeah, of course."

"Then you leave this table alone, eh."

"Yeah, no problem."

Jacob walked away from the table, hearing Frank explain to himself that he was new and didn't mean no harm.

"How about you go and take a break. Look, it's almost nine o'clock." Frank said as he went back into the office. Jacob glanced up to the antique clock and decided that a break was a good idea. He needed a few minutes to sort out the last two days and why this old man was so crazy about replacing that lightbulb.

Jacob went back to the bar counter and sat in one of the bucketseat stools. He reached down and pulled out a pack of half-mashed cigarettes. He found that no one was smoking, so he raised his cig so that Frank could see it. He gave Jacob a slight gesture that it was all right to light up. Jacob struck the match and held it protectively to the still unlit end of his tobacco stick. He took a puff, then another, then another; until the receiving end of his tobacco was red hot. He watched the lit paper; the way the smoke curled around him and then he let it escape upward to the high rafters. It was the first cigarette that he'd smoked, having bought the pack three months ago. The smoke made him want to gag; it choked him every time he tried to inhale. They didn't taste like he thought they would, but he figured he had saved them for this moment, so he would just get to like it. Kinda like black olives.

Chapter 5

His Reflection

Jacob could see his reflection in the momentous mirror behind the bar, darkly lit up by the light shining through the countless bottles of booze.

"You worked here long?" Jacob asked as Frank made himself a drink.

"I've been here since they opened the doors. 1921."

"What did you do when you started out?"

"What's with all the questions? You a cop?" He stared at him, his hand now wrapped around Jacob's drink, waiting to send him packing.

"No, just a writer having a bad day." Jacob smiled back, enjoying the idea of calling himself a 'writer.'

"Well, if you ain't a cop you're welcome to stay."

"Thanks." The young writer lifted his drink, a free soda pop, to his lips and toasted Frank silently.

Jacob wanted to tell him about his novel, how it was about a homicide detective from the big city who moves out to a farming town to solve crimes. Jacob had worked on it for months, but it had stopped being interesting and it was now a burden. He had painted himself into a corner with the character, all because he was trying to write about something he had no experience or love for. Jacob, after thinking of this, did not want to mention his novel. It was at Jilly's house; soaking wet with the ink now washed away. He didn't have the heart to toss the manuscript out before leaving Bishop Springs, so he allowed it to be ruined as he stood out in the Arcadian rain.

"What do you think of this idea for a book?" He went through the synopsis of the story and Frank listened closely. When he had finished, Frank said, "I think it would get old real quick. Besides, what do you know about the criminal life?" He knew that he'd hurt the boy's feelings but he trusted that it was the truth and the boy would learn from it. He nodded and went to the other end of the counter. Jacob slowly spun to his left on his swiveled barstool, eyeing over the couples in the dimly lit room, his feelings bruised and he didn't expect it to sting so much.

They were laughing and talking to each other, occasionally looking up at the old clock on the wall and then down to their wrist watches. Jacob turned his focus back on the soda in front of him and the half-eaten bowl of peanuts to his left. He reached over, sifted through the empty shells, and found one without someone else's fingerprints. He broke the shell open and scooped out the nutty inside, feeling the slight sting of the salt on his lips. Jacob pushed his finger back into the bowl and stirred it until he found a few more.

He put the newly cracked shells in his mouth and sucked the salt off them, letting the unique taste mix with the already present soda pop and cigarette.

Jacob spun back around and leaned forward, grabbing a napkin from a stack resting near the salt shakers, wincing from the awful cigarette taste. He then found the stomach to return to his seat and wiped his salty mouth.

Chapter 6

▼

Finishing Off A Bottle

Jacob finished the soda and then put his hand into his pocket. Inside were his last three bucks. Jacob was shivering from the cold dampness of the evening air. He was more than willing to spend his remaining money on some scotch to get himself warm.

Frank saw the crumpled money on the bar and came over.

"Here, put your money away kid, you look like you need those three bucks." Jacob laughed to himself, finding it funny that he had lost his twenty dollar bill, after all those opportunities to treat himself on the trip getting to Arcadia. Frank came over with another soda pop. Jacob asked him if he could have a single of scotch. Frank shook his head 'no', then poured the scotch. He placed the glass in the seat next to Jacob and he turned his back. Jacob reached over and took the glass.

"You underage?" Frank asked loudly with his back to Jacob. Then he whispered to the kid to say 'no.' Jacob did and Frank was back to looking at him.

"Just don't drink it when I'm over here, okay? You're not driving are you?"

"No sir."

"What did I say about that sir stuff?"

"I forgot Frank. Thank you for the soda." Jacob winked. Frank just chuckled to himself, as he cleaned the glasses behind the counter.

"Can you work full time?"

"Sure that isn't a problem."

"Good. You got a place to stay?"

"With my cousin, it's on the other side of town."

"Tell you what. Don't go home until after last call."

"You got it." Jacob could see the bottle of scotch that Frank had poured his drink from and it was nearly gone. Frank dumped the remaining liquor into Jacob's glass, watching for anyone to see him do it. Jacob thanked him, but Frank just said he was, "finishing off a bottle."

He didn't think Frank was used to a compliment; that was a shame, because Jacob thought the old guy was cool once he got past that whole butcher knife thing.

Jacob lifted the short glass to his mouth. The vapors that came off the liquid, caught him off guard.

"Scotch is good for getting a fella warm," his dad would often say. Too bad he never said what it tasted like.

Jacob was kept company at the bar railing with the auburn colored glass of scotch. He breathed in through his mouth, as he saw the smoke vent from his nose. Jacob's posture became more lax as he grew more comfortable with the smoke and the alcohol; for the first time in a long time, he was happy for his own reasons.

He sipped his drink, dissecting its flavorable warmth with every swallow. He could feel it running down his throat and then the heat spread to the tips of his toes and the far ends of his fingers. Jacob was warm from the inside out.

"I think I found my new favorite drink." He said to Frank.

"Hope not. That stuff's ten dollars a glass."

Jacob choked for a second, his body reacting to the luxury of the rich. Jacob wasn't used to such comfort, but damn, it was sure getting used to him.

Following that short break, they worked the rest of the night without much going on. The young barback learned how to run the register and how to bus-tables. Jacob was laughing to himself, causing Frank to come over with a strange look on his face and asked him what he was doing.

"I was just remembering this story that a guy on the farm told me."

He looked up, checked the busy faces of the other patrons and he slid back down to Jacob's end of the bar.

"Oh yeah? Well I've got stories that'll put hair on your ass."

He had a devilish grin on his face, as if Jacob was a rabbit walking into a bear trap.

"You ever heard of Mr. Crane?" Frank asked, arms folded and facing Jacob.

"Never." Jacob replied.

"He's the Boogie Man in a black suit...." The hook was in. Jacob took a big gulp of the scotch and made himself comfortable. He loved a good story; especially one that didn't involve a farmer, a broken tractor, and a pig named 'Dwight.'

As he hung there in suspense, Frank looked at him then laughed. He had put one over on Jacob.

"Before we start telling stories, how about you take out the garbage and sweep up?" Jacob jumped up to do as he was asked, finishing in a quick flurry of broom strokes. Frank announced last call and within a few minutes, Jacob's first evening of work was over.

"Here kid, this is the key to the room upstairs. It's nothing fancy but it'll keep you dry and warm."

"Thanks Frank. I really appre...."

"Yeah, just don't burn the damn place down." That said, Frank and Jacob walked outside and the door was locked behind them.

"Good night kid," Frank said, waving the back of his hand as he got into his car. Disappointed that Frank forgot about telling him the story, Jacob answered back, as he approached the mossy steps, "Night Frank."

Chapter 7

▼

The Lonely Broom

Jacob stumbled up the slippery steps, right up to the locked door and musty smell. He put the key in and pushed the door. It wouldn't open. Jacob gave it a pull then just started shaking the handle. He could hear someone walking up the alleyway, coming right towards those mossy stairs and him. He jiggled the key; with a shot of panic, the door flew wide open. A rush of warm, dank air came out. Jacob stepped into the room, flung his jacket on the floor, and locked the door behind him.

With the footsteps in the alley unable to come in, he pushed aside the dusty lace curtains and opened the windows. A breeze came in and flushed the one-room palace clean. The room was already warm from the radiant water heater under the window, making the cooler breeze not so unbearable.

Jacob checked out the kitchen and the bathroom areas. He found a payphone mounted on the wall, so he picked up the receiver and found a live line. He put his fingers into his pocket and retrieved the last of the Minnesota quarters. He dropped the coins into the slot and punched in Jilly's number. She picked it up and was happy to hear he had a job. He told her the bad news that he wouldn't be living with her. For some reason, there really wasn't a sound of disappointment, at least not like he expected. They arranged to meet up in the morning so Jacob could get his things. She yawned quite a bit during the call so he wrapped it up with a genuine, "night cousin."

He stretched out on the army cot that was left by the last tenants. In patting the bed material with his hands, he caused a dust cloud to rise. He coughed and gagged as the taste of the crud landed in his open mouth. He eventually stopped choking, sitting there thinking about his day and allowing himself to slowly go to sleep.

The next morning, he woke up to the sound of Frank pounding on the door.

"Hey kid, we got work in ten minutes. Hope you're up!"

"Yeah Frank, just on my way down." He said still wiping the sleep boogers from his eyes and trying not to sound so tired.

"I'll see you downstairs then."

"All right Frank...." Jacob laid his head back down, scrunching his face into the pile of rags that he used as a pillow. He yawned and shook off the sleepiness; his clothes were over at Jilly's, so he'd have to wear the ones from the day before. He wasn't worried, no one would notice.

He put his clothes back on and ran down the steps, nearly breaking his neck on a puddle of water. Jacob jogged into the bar to find a small group of people meeting in a cluster.

"What's this?" He asked Frank.

"The local commerce club, they meet here every Thursday."

"Oh, well what can I do?"

"You can start by not wearing the same clothes. But since you're already here, the hell with it." So much for no one noticing.

That morning was slow, even when Jacob was running back and forth with the club's coffee mugs and boxes of donuts. He enjoyed the chitchat of those rich people and was happy to just be around them. He didn't understand why such well to do people would meet in such a working mans' bar. Frank said they all started in the neighborhood and then got rich. They liked to come back to the old stomping grounds, to remember when it wasn't all about the money.

It wasn't even their fancy clothes or elitist speech that interested Jacob. It was their wallets. The knowledge that they could buy whatever they wanted whenever they wanted, was a potent drug to his farmboy mind. Sure, his folks weren't poverty-stricken but that doesn't mean dick, at least not in Bishop Springs. His dad made some risky choices, namely the decision to stay on the farm and not sell when they had the chance. The only reason they weren't foreclosed is that the farm was never mortgaged. They had owned that land since the turn of the century and the only governmental money that they had to come up with was taxes.

Jacob got to watch his chance for going to college get flushed down the toilet because his father wouldn't allow Jacob to sell his portion of the land. It had been left to Jacob in his grandfather's will, but it made Doyle the executor until Jacob turned 25. That was during Jacob's junior year in high school and instead of filling out college applications and checking on dorm living, he gave up the fantasy of being more than a farmer's son.

Doyle even gave him a speech about earning his own money for college, that he should do it for the experience. That was funny to Jacob because he would have prepared for his college tuition ahead of time, if it weren't for Doyle's stubbornness about making him a farmer.

Getting back to the matters of the bar, Jacob tried to not to concern himself with that darkened booth, as it tempted his mind all morning and into the rest of the day. That afternoon was slower, with people coming in to have a drink or just talk. He spent most of the day sweeping up dust that had blown in from the street.

"You should see this place in July. Whoa!" Frank shouted, making Jacob picture the bar buried under a dust cloud.

"You should call this place the pig-pen." Frank just looked at him.

"What are you trying to say boy?" He looked back at Jacob.

"Nothing Frank, just fooling around."

"That broom over there's getting mighty lonely." He slid over to the dustpan and broom and kept his mouth shut. Jacob spent the rest of the day like that, and lucky for him, the broom didn't have anything interesting to say.

Chapter 8

▼

Mr. Winston's Bad Day

Once the last of the customers had stumbled out of the door, Frank gave Jacob an ice water, with lots of ice and no straw. Then he took a seat next to his new employee at the bar rail.

"You remember what I said last night? About me knowing stories?"

"Yeah."

"Well how'd you like to hear one of them?" Jacob sat back with his glass of water in hand and gave him a welcome salute. Frank took a gulp of his scotch and then began to speak.

"Way back…I'm talking 1950's…right at the hay day of organized crime up here, there was this mobster called Mr. Winston. He and his crew would drive up here from Chicago and would take over the Safari Inn. He brought all his own booze, broads, and bullets. He loved the Safari Inn, for its knotty pine walls and the circular shape of the main room. He'd tell the owners that he was going to take over for the summer. They didn't have the guts to say no. This guy had everything in town wired. If he needed anything, he had it in a matter of minutes. I'm talking anything."

"Cool." Jacob said.

Frank just looked at him, a little bothered his reaction would be so stupid, but he dismissed it and moved on.

"Mr. Winston had men in Arcadia to take care of things before his arrival. They got his house and the Safari Inn ready, even taking care of his mail. That's how the letters were missed at first. Mr. Winston's men just took his packages and letters and locked them in a safe until he got there to tend to them. Mr. Winston arrived in town and settled in. A few days go by and he decides to check out his mail. Well, there were catalogs and little gifts from friends and family. Then at the bottom of the pile was a bundle of black envelopes with white lettering that was addressed to the 'soon-to-be-dead Mr. Winston.' He opens them with his silver dagger letter-opener and reads. Beginning with the first word all the way to the unreadable signature, the letter promised that he'd be dead within the month. The first letter was dated a month before, so he figures that the deadline on these threats is coming up. He starts getting very nervous because no one's ever had the balls to threaten him like that. He hired a whole squad of local goons and told them to find out who'd been sending those letters. He didn't know how this stalker knew him, since he had just arrived from Chicago two days before.

The goons went out and questioned some of their street contacts and it turned out, someone had seen a young man putting envelopes, just like the ones with the notes, into a nearby mail box. These goons have about a brain between them, so they decide to stakeout the mailbox and if the kid comes again they'd rough him up. A few hours go by and nothing. They start getting all antsy; so they start up the banged up Cadillac they were in and leave. Just as they pass by the box, one of them sees this kid walking towards them on the sidewalk, right in the general direction of the mailbox. They pull over and look back through the rear window and sure enough that kid, probably around 13 or 14, puts a stack of letters in the mail slot and runs off. They figured they got their man."

"They go into Mr. Winston's club and tell him everything they've seen. He just laughs right in their faces and kills the leader of those morons for lying to him. The rest of them are so scared that they don't say another word about the kid. They back away and were in the Cadillac parked outside before Mr. Winston could blink. One of the thugs convinced the others that the kid had to be braced or rubbed out. If they braced him, they'd just scare the kid into stopping the letters. Moreover, if they whacked him, it would prove the kid was responsible for the threats or knew who was. But they couldn't just pop some kid and then go back in the club with some dignity. They knew it had to be up to Mr. Winston. If he said, 'pop him,' then it wasn't a problem. With their balls intact, they drove off in search of the kid.

Everyone they questioned had the same answer; 'I don't know any kid.' Everyone but Mr. Goula, who was a baker and small-time scum bag. He had gambling debts with Mr. Winston, so he made a deal with the thugs; he gave them the kid-they paid his debts. They agreed and the baker went back inside his shop and made a call. About five minutes after the call was made, a kid comes around the corner. It was the same one who put the earlier letters into the mailbox.

They grabbed him and tossed him into the awaiting car. The Cadillac sped off, leaving a cloud of exhaust and burnt rubber smoke behind them. As they hurried across the deserted streets, they checked the time and it was only Midnight. Mr. Winston would definitely be at the club; they could deal with the kid that night.

The kid, who didn't say a damned thing the whole time, just stared blankly into the front seat. They looked at him, wondering if he was crazy or something. The boy said nothing. They screamed at the kid, telling him they'd break his legs if he ever wrote another letter to Mr. Winston. Still, the kid just sat there. They went so far as to point a gun in the boy's face, but he did nothing."

Chapter 9

▼

Always Leave Them Wanting More

"The Cadillac tore down M-22, until it made a left turn on Safari Inn Drive. The dark dirt road was lined with wooded lots and ended in a dead end. They got out and took the kid down a two-track pathway, which led them to the club. They arrived at the club, with the music blaring and the women dancing. Mr. Winston's crew lined the back wall ready for battle. The group of bungling thugs brought the kid in through the dance floor, past the bar and over to a door in the back.

The guards of Mr. Winston's only let the boy in, having heard what the thugs had said; figuring the boy wasn't a threat. Mr. Winston sat in the back office, a blonde-haired woman on his arm and a pile of uncounted money in front of him. He told the boy to sit, then asked him if he was the letter writer. The boy nodded 'yes.' The gangster stood up, reaching into his pocket and pulled out his .45, emptying the clip with his thumb, as he stepped towards the boy. He kept walking, until he had passed the boy and locked the office door from the inside. He had left one round in the magazine.

The gangster returned to the table and sat opposite from the kid, placing the pistol on top of the money.

"There's one bullet in there. One for you or one for me. You think you're gonna kill me? I didn't think so. You want anything before I shoot your stupid little ass?"

The kid looked up at him, for the first time showing signs of life.

"Yeah, I want you to pack up your things and never come back."

"Oh yeah?" The mobster asked sarcastically.

"Yeah, and I want to thank you." He nonchalantly said.

"For what?" The crooked gangster asked.

"For getting me in here. I never could have gotten this close to you by myself. Not only that, but Mr. Goula owes me a favor now: for getting his debts erased. The rest of the town owes me too."

"What'd you do for them?" The gangster chuckled to himself as he angled his body back to reach the one-shot pistol.

When he turned around, there was the boy sitting plain as before, but now holding a fully loaded .45.

"I got rid of you," the boy said as he fired, not allowing Mr. Winston to speak. The bullets tore through the expensive suit and made a popping sound throughout the room. The men outside the locked office stomped and smacked the steel body of the security door.

The blood ran out of the mobster's chest and stomach, one pool being nearly black from where a bullet had gone into his liver. As he stood there with the smoking barrel and blood on the ground, the kid felt better. He stretched his fingers and arms, and then put the uncounted cash into a bag that was lying near the table.

"Here. You didn't see anything." The kid tossed a stack of bills to the blonde. He walked over to the body of Mr. Winston and wiped up some of the blood, using the handkerchief from the slain mobster. He wiped some of the blood on the protesting blonde, and then he held it up to the wall. His job now done, he loaded up everything and was gone. Escaping out some secret passageway he knew about, having gone to the library and studied the blueprints of that club. The boys outside the door couldn't get in; the bloodied-up blonde couldn't escape yet.

After breaking through the not-so-secure mortar wall, Mr. Winston's guards looked inside the back room. What they found inside is the stuff of gangland myth. Right over the body of their dead boss, was a name drawn in the blood of Mr. Winston. They looked at each other, all secretly hoping to never again see the name of 'Mr. Crane' again. They told the blonde how to unlock the security gate and escorted her out. They just needed to leave that club, to leave it far behind. They got what they wanted, because a small group of the villagers poured gasoline on the building and waited for the signal from the dangerous young man. When the partygoers were out, the kid tossed a flaming Zippo lighter onto the combustible puddle and watched as their little mobster retreat went up in flames. The gangsters that escaped never came back."

Frank smiled at Jacob, letting him know the story was over, following in that great story-telling tradition of 'always leave em wanting more.'

"So did they ever catch him, the kid?"

"I'll tell you in a minute." Frank walked over to some customers who had come in minutes prior; taking their orders rather quickly. Probably because they had been sitting there waiting for him to finish the story. Thirst, not mobsters, was all that they were interested in.

Jacob tossed back the rest of his water and decided not to drink anymore. It was best to stop now, or he'd have to pee in the middle of Frank's next story.

Chapter 10

▼

Lucky New Years

He slid out of his chair and went into the restroom. He pulled the saloon style doors open and took his position over the porcelain bowl. His actions after that point must be left to your imagination, though it can be told that he came out whistling. He resumed his seat and now took small sips from his new glass of water.

He spent the next minutes thinking about the story of 'Mr. Crane versus Mr. Winston,' intent on romanticizing it until it was truer than true. The bar started to empty, which was not a big surprise for a weeknight. He waited for Frank to finish getting the patrons' drinks and to get back to his drop-dead stories.

In the main part of the bar, was a wall covered by framed photos. One read, "Lucky Joe-Happy New Year-1931." Through the hazy shot of all those party goons, was Lucky Joe, the man with the scar.

Mr. Lucky Joe had a martini in one hand and the prettiest girl in the room on the other. In the very far-right corner, there was a booth with no light above it. Jacob squinted and stared but couldn't make out who it was. Frank came up to him and asked what he was doing.

"Who's this man? Is he Lucky?" Jacob turned towards the old man with interest.

"No, that was someone else …you've got an eye for the good stories." He said as he walked towards the bar.

"So? Who was he?"

"You sure you want to hear this? It's pretty bloody stuff?" He doubted Jacob's ability to hear such true-life grit.

"I think I'll manage." He replied.

"Okay. That right there, is Mr. Crane," he said while pointing to the photo.

"That's impossible…you already said Mr. Crane was 13 or 14 back in the 50's. How could he be in a picture taken in 1931?"

"Just because they got the same name, don't make them the same person."

"What?" Jacob asked totally confused. Frank leaned in and looked around before continuing.

"Just about three people know what I'm about to tell you, so if you say a damn word to anybody else about it, I'll find you."

"Okay, I promise."

"There have been ten or so, Mr. Cranes. If you could imagine a contract killer, someone of professional status unlike any other assassin, that's Mr. Crane."

"The first one was in the middle 1800's. From what I hear, he's supposedly the one who got the gun for John Wilkes Booth. No less than one-thousand people have been killed by Mr. Crane."

"I still don't understand," Jacob said.

"Mr. Crane, the first one, got too old to do his job, so he took on a pupil. He went to an orphanage and got a kid that had been mistreated and neglected. He taught the kid how to fight, survive, plan, and kill. After a decade or so passed, the time came when the teacher was too weak and vulnerable to his enemies. The student had the responsibility to kill his master. It was done out of respect; it was an act of honor. Mr. Crane gave the student a golden bullet, one with the kanji character for peace engraved in it. The student then loaded his weapon with the golden projectile and pointed the muzzle at the temple of his masters' head. With a promised smile, he pulled the trigger.

After the teacher was dead, the student took on the identity of Mr. Crane."

"So really, Mr. Crane could live forever."

"Yep." He answered, with a slight gesture of urgency.

"What about kids? Were the men allowed to have families?"

"No, that's part of the rules. No kids—no wife- no loved ones of any kind."

"How do you get your family to forget you?" Jacob asked.

"Listen, the last thing in the training was the students' acceptance of the rules. If he didn't agree, he got a bullet in the brain. As for the family, the kid was an orphan. He had no family. If he happened to have friends, the student and teacher would involve the local cops and just fake his death."

"So, is there a Mr. Crane still running around?" Jacob joked, unaware of Franks' concerned thoughts.

"Look Mack, if you're gonna screw around with this I might as well shoot myself in the head. Understand?" His face was covered with tiny beads of sweat and his eyes were nearly bulging out at Jacob.

"I understand." Jacob answered with newly found seriousness.

"Good, now I'll continue. Back when that picture was taken, Mr. Lucky Joe came to Arcadia for some rest and relaxation. Back then this place was a speakeasy in the middle of prohibition. Arcadia was a popular pick-up site for illegal booze. With the harbor so close, the men out of work, and the lack of cops, the mobster's loved it up here. They couldn't spend their money fast enough. Everyone in town that ran a business gladly paid into the protection racket they had going during the summers. You had to, or they'd break your kneecaps. These are rare photos, special ones to me. I bought these pictures from the old owner. I was the errand boy for the place, so I might be in some of these shots. Most of this place is the same, except for the office in the back. There were these big steel doors painted god awful black."

"The first owner was this great old guy, who used the place as a bait shop before the great depression, but had to shut it down since no one had any money. Faced with losing his business, he chose to make it a nightclub, painting the front windows black and blocking up the front door with a layer of bricks. If you were to pass by, you would have sworn that this building was the elevator to Heaven before thinking it was a booze filled nightclub. In no time, the old fella was making money hand over fist. That is, until the village's 'protectors' wanted a piece of the action. They came into the place waving their guns around, touching the women like they owned the place. Just when the old fella couldn't take it any more, a then unknown man stepped up to the head thug. The two other goons put their hands on their guns and waited for an order to shoot. The leader just smiled into the face of the tall-lanky man, who before getting up, didn't say two words to anybody. The mysterious man spoke in a low almost unheard voice causing the thug to lean in to hear. The crowd looked to the thug, hoping his face would tell them what was said.

The thug boss told the others to put their guns down. They didn't listen. The tall-lanky stranger, dressed all in black, grabbed the thug boss and broke his neck. Right there, in the middle of a crowded dance floor and in front of hundreds of unbelieving eyes, he stood there totally calm and didn't even break a sweat. The other two men froze from seeing their boss killed so easily. The stranger told them to take the body with them, but they were too proud to just walk away.

The bigger of the two drew his weapon, but the thin killer was already in the process of breaking his arm. The crisp break made a sound like celery being snapped. The other thug was able to get a shot off before the stranger grabbed the silver handgun and directed the barrel into the doomed thug's mouth. The three-mobster wannabe's were dragged out into the street and were run over by uncaring pedestrians and paid off cops.

The party music was struck up again and the mystery man quietly walked to his booth in the back of the bar. Now that the attention of the room was on him, he reached up to the lamp over his booth and turned it off. Right before the light went out, the old owner could see a scar stretch down the length of the forearm. Maybe another disagreement?

Feeling in awe of the spectacle that he witnessed; Mr. Lucky Joe walked up to the black suit garbed man and began a conversation. The two of them talked until the early morning, Mr. Lucky Joe looked like he needed some sleep. But the man in the shadows tipped his hat to the exiting mob boss and then escorted himself through the black door in the back and out through some secret way."

"When was the picture taken?" Jacob asked.

"Right after the three men were killed." Frank pointed to a small smudge of pink and white on the dance floor, which it turns out, was the hands of the three dead men.

"After those men were killed, no one messed with this place again."

"Even today?" Jacob leaned back in disbelief.

"Even today." Frank said confidently.

Jacob let out a deep breath that seemed to be in him for the last twenty minutes, being held hostage by his anxious listening.

"Want me to teach you how to make a Nothing Special?" Frank asked from the other end of the counter.

"What's in it?"

"Nothing Special." He started laughing, having set Jacob up for a corny but funny joke.

"Sure, why don't you show me?" He said off the cuff as Frank walked from the photos and went behind the counter. He tightened his apron strings and grabbed a clean glass for the drink they were about to make.

"I better clear my palette Frank." Jacob was walking to the restroom again.

"Your palette? What are you talking.. Oh I see. Just make sure you wash them hands. I mean it." Jacob pushed the door open and stepped up to the urinal. He went through the motions and was finished in seconds. He turned on the faucet, washing his hands, then his face. He looked up to his reflection in the dirty mirror and watched the drops roll off his nose and into the sink below him. He dried his hands on the paper towel and went back to work.

Chapter 11

▼

Heritage Days 1980

Jacob climbed back into the still warm barstool and yawned. He had gotten rid of most of the ice water, but he was still suffering the effects from not eating lunch. The bar was finally quiet, with no jukebox to strike up the tempo, no dance floor for him to sweep.

"Hey, you want something to eat? I'm gonna get some grub from down the street. They'll have it here in 15 minutes." Frank said with the phone in his hands.

"That sounds great, but, I don't have any money."

"Don't worry about it. I'll just take it out of your pay." He was laughing but Jacob wasn't sure if he was joking.

"Okay, then I'll have what you're having."

"Pasties and grits it is." Frank spoke into the phone and made the order. Jacob had never eaten a pastie or a grit; he'd never wanted to try a pastie or a grit. Chalk it up to having a growling stomach.

Now Frank had told Jacob some gruesome tales, describing the very mysterious Mr. Crane. Were they true? Why would Frank put himself in such danger, gossiping about someone so lethal? Why would this bartender and owner, of obvious experience and common sense, talk so openly about such a criminal?

Jacob looked Frank in the eyes and asked him, "are you bullshitting me?"

"Why do you ask?" Frank replied with genuine wonder.

"How could you know so much about him?" Frank didn't know what to say. He started to speak but the words weren't there. His eyes moved from side to side, as if he were mentally sorting out his answer, checking to see if he'd be put to death if he answered wrong.

"We better just leave it alone...it's for the better."

Jacob didn't want to, but the nervous way Frank was acting made him not push it any further.

Jacob picked up a tray that had a pitcher of Frank's special drink and some glasses on it. He strolled over to the waiting customers. They accepted the frosty glasses and the unique drink with thirsty appreciation, drinking it down before the sides of the glass could sweat cool droplets of water. Their fingerprints showed on the melted sections where their warm fingers had held the glass.

Above their heads was the wall of fame that had photographs of famous people who had visited the bar. Jacob even found photos of the 'Rat Pack' in their prime.

"What's the deal with this one?" He asked, pointing at a medium sized frame.

"That one is of Heritage Days 1980."

"What's so special about Heritage Days of 1980?" He said walking away from the wall, over to his barstool, then carried his drink, over to a booth closer to the wall.

"That's when the Middle Street Gang moved into town. That's when things got bloody. We used to get a lot of 'connected' guys in here, just drinking or chasing women. Nothing big. Only catch with those types was you had to respect them no matter what. I knew that, everyone else seemed to. Then one night we had a problem with respect. A big shot executive at a lumber company was in here complaining about how lazy his clearing-crew was. They'd been out in the woods, off and on for two years and still hadn't cut down the trees they needed. The executive was talking big, making all kinds of stupid threats and impossible promises. Well after about thirty minutes of hearing his yap, one of Tommy 'the bow-legged' Gabberini's boys comes up to the exec's table. This man tells the drunken executive to shut his mouth and just be a good little boy.

Apparently the guy didn't know who this man was, cause when the thug got done speaking, the exec makes his hand like a sock-puppet and starts mocking him. He even had the Italian Mafioso accent going. He was making cracks about pasta and car trunks, he had everyone laughing. Everyone but Tommy 'The bow-legged' Gabberini. He just sat there with that serious look on his face. I came over to the table and told the boys not to pay him no mind, that I had just called the cops to come and take that bastard away. Tommy looked up from the table right at me, and then down at his Rolex.

'If this citizen ain't gone or quiet in the next minute, he's gonna be dead. Understand?'

'Certainly, Mr. Gabberini.' That was it. We had to shut him up, or that gangster was gonna kill him. I told Denise, a friend of mine at the time, to go over to the restaurant down the street and get Jim Yagger, a friend of mine. He was a big guy who moonlighted as a bouncer at the Cabbage Shed in Elberta.

He came over and asked the exec to walk out. The exec refused. Mr. Gabberini was counting the seconds, even going to the point of holding onto his bodyguard's arm in order to give the man his due time. Well time ran out, and even through the pleadings of my buddy Jim, one of Tommy's boys put a gun in the exec's mouth and pulled the trigger.

There was nothing. Not a pop or a shot. The barrel was empty. The exec pissed his pants on the spot, then collapsed. I thanked Mr. Gabberini for his mercy. He said he meant for the gunman to kill him, but they didn't want to waste a bullet on such a piece of garbage. Still I thanked him up and down the bar, escorting he and his men out of the side entrance. I had Jim toss the exec out of the bar and heard him swearing at me all kinds of threats. 'I'm gonna kill you, you mother!' I came in and closed the bar an hour early, I needed to get myself together. The silence helped me to brush off the insults and stay safe. The whole night replayed in my head and I realized just how close I came to witnessing another murder."

"So what does that have to do with Mr. Crane?" Asked a drowsy eyed Jacob.

"It's got everything to do with him. The exec that got the piss scared out of him hired Mr. Crane for a job. He was supposed to find the thug that put the gun in the exec's mouth and make an example of him. Now five years go by since that Heritage Day celebration, and finally Mr. Crane decides to hit the guy. But killing a foot soldier in a Mafioso family is like whacking an ice cream man. It doesn't take any skill. Mr. Crane decided to make a real example, using Mr. Gabberini as the target. A few weeks passed but nothing was heard or seen from Mr. Crane. Word on the street spreads that the Crane hit rumor is just gossip. Still Mr. Gabberini waits. He stays indoors, sleeps with a loaded pistol, and has food tasters to check his food. All in the desperate attempts at staying alive. Weeks continue to pass until Mr. Gabberini starts getting relaxed, thinking the hit rumor was bullshit. He gets dressed up, calls up his boys and goes out to eat. 'Pasta by the Creek' was the name of the joint and Tommy ordered a big meal and a bottle of wine. He was known for his knowledge of fine wines and always prided himself on it. The appetizers were on the table and the wine just poured, so he stood up in the back of the restaurant feeling totally comfortable and secure.

He made a mock toast to Mr. Crane, saying something about his lack of courage and small balls. Either way, when he sat down to eat, he raised his wineglass up to his lips, looked down the goblet of crystal, and saw what he thought was a familiar face. He knew the face but couldn't place it. He nudged the boys to go and see who it was. He returned to his chair and reclined back, not paying attention to the kitchen door to his left."

Chapter 12

▼

Always Out of Sight

"The door opened and a few waiters came out with food in tow. When the door opened again, a tall-lanky man wearing a black suit came out. The mystery man did a kick to Mr. Tommy's face, purposely aiming at the propped up wineglass. It caused death instantly as the sharp bits of glass were shoved into the mouth and face of Tommy Gabberini. The bodyguards heard the thud as Mr. Tommy hit the table face first. It was too late. You might ask, 'why kick the glass? Why not just shoot him?' Well, normal contracts wouldn't have told Mr. Crane how to do his job. That contract wasn't his average type of kill. That job was very personal. Not to Crane, but to the executive. There had to be an inevitable feeling of revenge. The police would later find pieces of glass in the parking lot and bloodstains from Mr. Tommy, but not a single footprint from the murderer. That was Mr. Crane's specialty. It was said that he could walk up to you wearing boots while crossing a field of eggshells, and still you wouldn't hear him. Trust me, everyone in town was on their best behavior, after that gross dining experience. Rumor has it that there was one last target on the executive's contract. Only Mr. Crane knows who it is and when he's gonna finish it."

"What does he look like, aside from being skinny and tall?" Jacob asked.

"It was a longtime ago, last time I saw him. Back when he was always well-dressed and quiet."

"Really, when? When did you see him?" Frank stopped pouring his soda pop, and paid extra-close attention to Jacob.

"Back when that picture was taken." He pointed again, up to the wall of photos, directing Jacob to look at a frame that was always hidden by shadow, always out of sight.

"Who's it of?" He asked with his squinting eyes, trying to see what could be so secretive.

"Her." Frank retrieved a photo of his then fiancé, taking it down off the wall. It was taken just a year before her death.

"She knew Mr. Crane?" The question was making Jacob more nervous than Frank.

"Yep. He was a regular here, in fact he was such a good customer that I promised to keep his booth waiting for him. This was before she fell in love with him. She had dragged her feet the whole way with me but when I was out of the picture, she was more than happy to get married. He was going to leave town and take her away from all the old beefs and grudges. He was a good killer but just not husband material. My fiancé, Melissa, loved to sing and dance, she was a natural. She'd start and I'd never want her to stop. I called her my angel; my gift from Heaven. I miss her so much…"

"What…happened?" Jacob knew he was prying but his curiosity was in control.

"She got a gig singing for the Cabbage Shed, a real swanky spot over by Elberta. That's where they met. I guess the owner was late in paying Mr. Crane's client and he was sent there to collect. The man didn't have the money, so just following orders, Crane took him out behind the restaurant and held his gun to the mans' head. Melissa had just finished her set when she went outside to get some fresh air. She took a walk along the docks, watching the full moon and gazing at the stars. She could see across the harbor, over to Frankfort, where young couples were just leaving the Garden Theater, having seen a movie. The thumping sandals that she wore made hollow smacking sounds on the old boards, still walking toward the main pier. She stumbled onto the man about to lose his life and she started to scream. Mr. Crane had his pistol pressed firmly to his head, but when he looked up and saw that he had a witness, he knew he'd have to escape.

People would be looking for him, looking because my girl had to go for a walk. He couldn't shoot her because of the rules: No killing of women or children. He just tucked his pistol back into his holster and straightened his black tie. Melissa stopped screaming and just stared. He tipped his fingertip up to his eyebrow and gave a small gesture, a bit of a salute and a gesture of good-bye. He ran the length of the dock, until he was cornered with the harbor to his back and a mob of onlookers coming down the path. They had been dining out on the Cabbage Shed's terrace and came running when they heard Melissa's scream. The man, who was to be killed, was screaming hysterics about a crazy man looking to rob him and how his life was threatened.

Mr. Crane again drew his weapon and took aim. It must have been a good 65-70 yards away, but he steadied his arm and fired. The bullet ripped through the throat of the squealer, gushing blood all over the wooden planks of the dock. Some might say it was poetic. I'd say so. Anyways, Melissa ran to the end of the pier so sure he wouldn't hurt her, and it was there that he dove into the water below."

Chapter 13

▼

Absinthe and Sugar

"The cops came out and the divers went in, but nothing was found. The case was closed, since no one got a good look at the mysterious man. Melissa was smart, because she kept her mouth shut, and her eyes open. It was after she thought she saw him in the marketplace, in her classes, that she shared this part of the story with me. I was only your age, well maybe a little older. 'Round 24 or so. I was finishing up trade school and Melissa was in a hurry to start living. I always figured we'd get to leave together. Then a few days later, the same tall-lanky stranger from the dock strolled in and ordered a drink. Since I was out running errands, Melissa was tending the bar for me. She normally wasn't here; I didn't want her around this place. She grew up with her well-off parents and didn't know that Mr. Crane was notoriously lethal.

She took the Absinthe and sugar cube to the man; not quite sure of how she'd deal with seeing him again. He raised his hand and took out the bulb above him, creating a shadow just for him. She looked down to him, making eye contact with the man whom she'd seen commit murder. He looked back at her, letting her know that his memory was sharp as well. They didn't say anything, but nothing went misunderstood."

"She went back to the bar and did her job; wiping up the water spots and clearing glasses. She went back to refill his glass, but instead he offered a seat. She accepted and began talking with him."

"Right off the bat, she didn't censor her questions. If she wanted to know something, than damn it, she'd ask. It didn't matter to her that he was a killer; there was something unusual between them, and it was stronger than morality or common sense. They finished that first talk with a laugh and a handshake. I walked into the place just as it happened. My heart raced and pounded, seeing that filthy bastard making the moves on my girl. I ran over there and grabbed her by the arm. I guided her over to the counter and whispered my objections. She dismissed my anger as jealousy and told me so in front of him. I watched her face change all of a sudden, she looked at me then she looked at him. She scowled at me, she smiled at him. She let go of my hand and sexily sashayed over to his booth. Her beautiful hands reached deep into her pockets and pulled out a piece of paper with her address. She stared back at me, as if daring me to say something. But I knew better, because I could feel the evil eyes of that man boring down on me from behind that shadow."

"I flipped the bar towel onto my shoulder and tried to shrug the whole thing off. I couldn't. The thought of them together drove me nuts the rest of the night. I even took a drink after last call. I never did that. I went to bed upstairs, in the apartment that's yours now. I didn't want to come to work, since she'd spend 100% of her time messing with Mr. Crane. The flirtatious glances and bent over postures. She joined him at his table every day, although I kicked and screamed. I didn't want some hired gun dating my fiancé. All it took was some damned killer coming in here and getting my future bride in danger. It was after I realized just how friendly he was being to her that I confronted him.

He spoke in that low-tone and was surprisingly respectful. He said he just liked talking to Melissa and he wouldn't think of putting her in danger.

He finished his Absinthe and left. I didn't hear the bell ring on the door but when I turned to look at his table, it was empty.

He called her house and told her mother to tell her, to expect him at six o'clock that next night in his booth. Holding in true assassin form, he arrived an hour early, just in case of an ambush I suppose. I don't quite remember how he got in and out of the bar; I never heard his footsteps. The only way I'd know he was there was if I heard the clicking of his cigarette lighter."

"Melissa heard that familiar clicking and set her purse behind the bars' counter. I tried to grab her arm and tell her to sit at the bar, but she went into the corner booth, darkened to his liking, and it was there that I assume they exchanged a kiss. I walked up to the table and asked him why he wanted my girl. He turned to Melissa and asked her if he had done anything wrong. She said no, then kissed him again. At that time we were all pretty much the same age, but I felt like a damned little kid, having to watch that display. What could have made her turn away from me so quick?"

Chapter 14

▼

His Soon-to-be Bride

"Since he wouldn't give me an answer, I looked to the white powder residue in her nostril.

"You missed a spot," I said to her. She held a napkin to her nose and wiped away the evidence.

"So that's it. Nothing left to say, just go to hell?" I stormed out of the bar and tossed my apron in a trashcan. I was going to leave with nothing; no money, no degree. Just a broken heart, a pair of worn flannels and a head full of broken up common sense."

"A few days later the old owner of the bar found me and asked me to come back to work. He tried to give me relief by saying that Melissa hadn't been coming in with Crane lately. I got out of the chair I was in and ran downstairs to the bar. I had been listening to the music from the first floor for the better part of the afternoon. When I walked in the place it was hopping; the jukebox was belting out Motown soul and in that shadow-blanketed booth, sat Mr. Crane and his soon-to-be bride.

She had this huge ring on her finger; it glowed under the late evening light of electric lamps. I worked that night, for myself and for Melissa. I figured I'd prove her leaving me wouldn't destroy me. I'd let the music cheer me up, the cigar smoke to clear my mind, and the soft scent of powdery shampoo to torture me.

A couple of weeks passed, then there they were. Mr. & Mrs. Crane. They had gotten legally married but I knew Melissa and she had always wanted a church wedding. That whole scenario was a real kick to the nuts, let me tell you. I waited tables and took out garbage in order for me to buy her a tiny ring that I had found in a local jewelry shop. He bought her a chunk of ice without any feeling and that was okay with her. I know we weren't meant for each other but the idea of she and I was fun to dream over."

"Did they get married?"

"No. Melissa had arranged for the church ceremony but she didn't live long enough to see it through. It all happened the day of the wedding. I heard when and where it was going to happen, so I got dressed up as best as I could and made my way down to the chapel. There were white roses everywhere and a full orchestra playing the brides' march. I tried to get in, but the locked doors kept the two safe to make their vows. The priest went through the first steps of the ceremony, then asked them to kneel. Mr. Crane went down first then helped her. They held each other's hands and smiled. Though I'm sure she was high at the time, I really think she was happy. The orchestra changed the background music and the priest asked for objections. They smiled at each other, and then I heard the popping sound. Then pop, pop, pop. The blood sprayed onto the priest, then something ripped through him. His holy robes were shredded with a hailstorm of Teflon-coated bullets. The priests' blood darkened the white roses with it's burgundy hue. Melissa dropped down dead, Crane was terribly wounded. The musicians who were contracted to work the wedding weren't just there to play. They were packed with guns from feet to frown.

I ducked down below the window frame, since one of them ran to that window to check for cops. I waited until the lookout had moved then peeked back inside. Crane slid a 9mm out of his pant leg and nailed nine out of the ten assassins. That tenth one just waited for Crane to run out of ammo. Sure enough, that's what happened. Crane's pistol clicked and clicked with its empty barrel, while the surviving killer slowly approached. I ran to the fire escape and climbed to the second floor. I broke the window open and quickly jumped inside. The only piece of jagged glass left in the window cut my left arm near the shoulder, giving the blood a chance to escape.

I made my way down to the blood stained pews, just in time to pick up a pistol from one of the slain killers. I never shot a gun before, so I just pointed and then jerked the trigger back. I only remember firing once, but it turns out I emptied the entire clip into the tenth assassin. Crane covered his face with his hands and waited for the smoke to clear. I dropped the gun and panicked. I felt like I was going insane. I slipped into my fear for so long that it was the red-stained hand of Mr. Crane that brought me out of it. He looked me in the eyes and then looked over to Melissa. He turned his head away from me and then whispered, "you were right."

I nodded to him, and then we went out the back door with Melissa's body. I slipped her into the back seat of the black Limousine and watched Mr. Crane toss a pipe-sized canister into the church. He threw himself into the car and ordered the driver to step on it. We pulled away just in time, because the church turned into a fireball. Strips of broken glass and chunks of brick and mortar flew through the now dark air. A statue of Baby Jesus landed on the hood of the car, freaking the driver out to the point of tears. I sat in the back of that limo and patted Melissa's head. I looked over to Crane and wished I could swap his life for hers."

Chapter 15

▼

Made up Melodies

"What about Crane?"

"I didn't see him for some time. He took me out to his house and made me swear to keep quiet. He promised he'd kill me if I talked to anyone about it. So I kept quiet. If anyone knew that I had his face in my memory, I'd be tortured and forced to give him up. Then maybe, if they didn't get to him first, he'd grant me a quick death."

"Well if you've got to have something to look forward to..." Jacob said trying to make a joke of his comment.

"You'll see what I mean. There'll be times when you'll look to the worst case scenario and know it's the most painless."

"I hope I never know that." He said, then Frank walked the picture of his angel back over to the wall and kissed his hand then placed the kiss on the lips of her picture. Jacob saw a tear being wiped away.

After Frank and Jacob talked about Frank's lost love, they closed the place down for the night and went their separate ways. Jacob trudged up the steps to his place and found a dust bunny scurrying across the floor.

He tried to sweep them up but they moved too fast. He boiled some water on the hot plate and readied himself for bed. He dropped the tea bag into the boiling water then poured a good dose of it into his only mug. He dunked the bag repeatedly, then left it to steep.

He walked over to the payphone and called his folks again. He was looking to impress them with his new job and responsibilities. Despite his excitement and expectations, he got the answering machine. In less than 30 seconds, he told his happy news and then he hung the phone up to tend to his bedtime tea. The mug of hot chamomile and spearmint tea made his eyes warm and sleepy. He could feel the day's worries and tensions fade away. He squeezed in a teaspoon of honey, keeping the tea stirred so as to give the honey time to dissolve. Once it was gone, he licked his fingertips clean of the sticky honey and set the mug down on the floor underneath his cot.

The lights were already turned off so he rested there in his boxers. He loved the way the wind blew in through the windows and across his bed/cot. The tiny hairs on his arms and legs would stand up in unison, then lie back down. He'd hum to himself cute songs and made up melodies, leaving the rest of Arcadia to another lullaby night.

He fell asleep right after his tea kicked in and remained with closed eyes until 2:00 a.m. He heard his doorknob being jiggled, and then a kick to the handle made the door fly open. Three men rushed into the room and attacked him. Jacob was instantly on his feet. In boxers, he grabbed, kicked, punched, and jabbed at them. One had a monkey wrench in his hands and took a big swing towards him. Jacob ducked of course, then kicked him in the face. He hit the floor hard, right before the sound of the wrench clanking against his head was heard. The other two tackled Jacob, but had loose grips. He kneed the biggest one right in the mouth, seeing the blood start to run free as it carried the loose teeth onto the tile.

The third was trying to get a lamp to hit him with, but he tripped over his own untied shoelaces and fell flat on his face. Jacob stood there in his plaid boxers and breathed heavily. They glanced back at each other then ran out of the room, sliding down the wet steps, nursing their broken arms and bruised faces. "Bastards," he said to himself. He looked around and was sure nothing was stolen.

"What's there to steal anyway?" He propped the door back up and put the moth-eaten couch in front as a barrier. He climbed back into bed and protected his aching hands.

He woke the next morning to the sound of someone rummaging through his kitchen drawers.

"Freeze, I've got a gun!" Jacob yelled to the man.

"Oh knock it off, you don't have any damn gun." Old Frank said with such assurance.

"Damn Frank, you won't believe what happened last night."

"Let me guess, three guys kicked down your door and attacked you. But you were able to fight 'em off and send them on their way."

"Yeah, that's exactly right. How'd you know?"

"It's his way of testing you. It looks like you passed."

"Who?"

"Crane stupid." Frank answered him.

"What's he want with a barback? I didn't do anything to make him angry did I?"

"Yep. That's exactly what happened. He's gonna shoot you in the head because you wanted to change his booths' lightbulb."

Jacob stood there with his heart in his throat; the panic enveloped him as he saw Frank start to chuckle and he knew Frank was just joking.

Chapter 16

Unnerved Gentleman

"I'm just kidding…gees. A neighbor reported a robbery attempt to the cops and they called me because I own the building." Jacob let out a pent up gulp of air and smiled at Frank. He got himself ready for the day and ate the last of his leftover pizza. Jacob reached into the mini-fridge, pulled out a bottle of Open-Pit Bar-B-Q sauce, and poured its crimson color onto the cold morning pizza.

Frank shuddered from watching him eat it so he went outside. The door was still crookedly propped up but Frank told him to not worry about it. Jacob finished his breakfast and was happily on his way to work.

It had been three weeks since Jacob first arrived, still without a girl but relieved to be working. He was growing so accustomed to Arcadian life that he figured he'd never leave, knowing that he'd miss the manners and courtesy too much.

He strolled into the bar and went about his business of apron's and cleaning tables. Frank turned the old phonograph up and they listened to old time dance tunes. Ella Fitzgerald was singing her heart out, and then

Louis Armstrong belted out note after note. The music from back then was so much better, from the trumpets to the jazzed pianos. The trombones were capped and the drummers were stoked for another set. Jacob tapped his foot the best that he could and saw Frank moving to the beat. Everyone in the bar was feeling no pain; the seats started filling until there wasn't even standing room. They had the doors wide open and the fans working like nobody's business. The smoke swirled out the doorways and disappeared into the afternoon sky. Frank stopped dancing and busily filled drinks and lit cigars. The ladies of the club had come to dance and dance they did. The jiggling bodies and the hot sun made all the gents in the place unnerved.

There was a vibe to the place, like sexual tension on a grand scale. Then one by one, couples were paying their bill and were walking out as they stared at one another. They went out in droves and took the party with them.

"Over to another bar, to some distant club…." Frank yelled to Jacob, explaining to him why they were leaving. He seemed satisfied in the Big Apple playing a role in those people's party memories.

Jacob lost interest in the tunes, only tapping every other beat and went back to the monotonous task of clearing tables. The last of the party group left, so Frank turned the phonograph off, and they were again quiet. That was fine with Jacob, as he nursed the bruised hands and goose egg on his head with cold compresses. Frank just laughed to himself then said, "you sure don't look good."

"I don't feel good. I didn't think writing could be this dangerous." Frank thought it was odd to hear him say that. After all, Frank had never seen a notebook or journal, had never been asked for an opinion on a story. He never really believed that Jacob was a writer. Jacob's hands were callused and he never complained about work. Writers were prissy, with their corduroy jackets and elbow patches. He thought that Jacob was a new kind of writer, working with his body and his mind. Frank guessed that he was benefiting from Jacob's earlier years on the farm. Not even Jacob wanted to believe that he was a writer.

Frank and Jacob were wiping off tables and began talking again.

"Well Mr. Writer, What did you do to land yourself here?" Frank was baiting him to answer.

"I wanted to write," Frank just shrugged, not seeing the crime in that.

"It's your life right?"

"Yep."

"Then what's the problem?"

"The problem is I was raised to be a farmer, to pass on the family tradition."

"So what, you changed the tradition? I figured you'd done something like ran away from home to join the circus." He thought it was all very funny. Jacob didn't take any offense.

"The real problem was my dad. He didn't let me sell off my part of the farm to pay for my college tuition."

"You're shitting me!"

"I shit you not. He went against my grandpa's will, not approving my decision to sell. My grandpa left it to me, to do whatever I wanted with it."

"What happens to the land?"

"My dad gets to keep it until I'm 25, then I have it no matter what. But for right now, he's the executor and he'll never approve selling it."

"Why didn't you sue him?" Frank asked in amazement.

"Because he's my dad." He stood back and let out a big breath.

"Maybe you're not as green as I thought."

"I wouldn't go that far." Jacob comically walked into a door, pretending to have broken his nose. Frank let out that deep sounding chuckle and everything was right again.

Chapter 17

Killer Looks and Dangerous Intentions

"How about another story?"

"About Crane?"

"Of Course," Jacob answered.

"Click-click, Click-click. Crane walked into the office building without hesitant steps, gently going up to the sleeping guard who was leaning back in his chair. He walled up the laughter inside him, struggling not to roar with giggles. He placed the 9mm, with its silencer, next to the fat man's head. He could have pulled the trigger and just went about his business. Nevertheless, he didn't. That just wasn't his style. Instead, that rent-a-cop kept on snoring and Mr. Crane made his way to the elevator."

"The box rose quickly, the doors having shut to the sound of instrumental heavy-metal. Go figure. He tightened the silencer, checked his ammo, and cleared his nose with his handkerchief. The allergy season was getting to him, the pollen, and dust were uncomfortably high. He adjusted the black silk tie so nicely worn by him, standing in the center of the lift with nothing but killer looks and dangerous intentions."

"He reached the penthouse and was off before the elevator could ring. The two guards near the lift's doorway were dead before they knew it, while the men posted at the suite's door were on their way down the gold and marble hallway towards Mr. Crane. One of them knocked over a vase, tripped over its bulbous curves and knocked himself out.

Crane left him to the mercies of a concussion and focused on the lone-bodyguard at the end of the smoke-filled corridor.

"Slide the weapon to me, I won't kill an unarmed man," Mr. Crane yelled down to the shaking guard, "come on fella, this bastards not worth dying over…is he?"

"Hell no," the guard answered under his breath. The gun slid across the floor and stopped at Mr. Crane's feet.

"Now step out, slowly!"

He could see the out-reached arms of the man coming towards him. The guard's face was covered with sweat.

"I know you…you were in Grenada." The bodyguard said confidently.

Crane punctuated his sentence for him, putting a bullet in his forehead, hating to do it.

"Fool. You should have not been so chatty."

He stepped over the other men's bodies, until he was face-to-face with the penthouse suite entrance. He checked his watch and knew he had five minutes to work. He kicked the door and rushed in, securing a small sense of peace, as he found no one in the room.

"Come out right now…or I start shooting through doors." Nothing.

"How important is that lunch-box to you? Important enough to take a bullet for? I doubt it, but maybe I'm wrong. I guess we'll find out now."

He pointed the pistol to the linen closet and fired. Tiny chips of painted wood flew through the air. He could hear someone moving. He walked so nonchalantly to the apartment door and closed it then locked it.

He crept around the living room, constantly aware of the heavy breathing of his target.

"Come on buddy, quit wasting my time. The cops are going be here any second. If they get here before I get my job done, you're going to fit in that lunch box." The couch-cushions opened up and a sweaty old man with a pansy-sized pistol came out from hiding. Crane disarmed him as if he were taking a sucker away from a child.

"Mr. Mayrock I presume." He said with a sly grin.

Mr. Mayrock had stolen a rare piece of memorabilia from a charity auction, a piece that had been slated for sale in order to help a local orphanage. That really pissed Mr. Crane off. He grabbed him by the throat and walked him over to the balcony. The railing was narrow and not that far above his waist. He lifted Mr. Mayrock's old body onto the railing and held him leaning out over the long drop.

"What do you think you'll hit first? The pool? The parking lot? Or the flag pole?"

"Please don't…I'm sorry…it was a mista.…"

Chapter 18

On the Balcony

Crane didn't let him finish. He pushed him out a little further, Mr. Mayrock's fear growing to extremes.

"I said I was sorry…wasn't that enough?"

"Not by a long shot. So, here's what I'm thinking. You go to your bank tomorrow morning and withdraw all your money. You put $1,000.00 in each envelope and then you get on a bus. Doesn't matter what bus, unless you're too good to ride the bus?"

"No sir, the bus will be fine."

"Good, because you're going to get on that bus naked with your life's savings and try to give it away. If you don't give it all away, I'll find you and then I'll remind you. Understand me?" He shook his head up and down; his robe started to fly up from the high-rise draft.

"And for god's sake, start wearing underwear. That's nasty." Crane turned him around and made him get down on his knees. He crossed his ankles and counted out the combination to his safe. 05-20-77. Mr. Crane pulled the lever down, hesitantly opening the vault. He looked past the stockpile of cash and diamonds, ignoring it all for a rusty little Lone-Ranger lunch box.

"If you ever try to pull this sort of thing again, you're going to find out that not everyone in jail likes a naked man." With that whispered, He was gone."

"Mr. Crane dropped his two 9mm's, having worn latex gloves and did not want to give the cops an excuse to look for an unknown shooter. As far as they'd know, one of the guards went bad and tried to whack his client. The others just did their jobs. Everyone went home happy. He was pleased with himself, in that moment allowing the worst mistake to be made. He heard the click before he even saw the gun. The jumpsuit wearing, masked bandit had a .357 cannon pointed at the back of his head.

"Did you get the box?" Crane didn't answer.

"I said did you get the box?" Still he said nothing.

"Oh hell," he grabbed the satchel from Mr. Crane's left hand all the while eyeing his right.

"So what do you carry…or do you mind me asking?" He asked with a smartass tone.

"9mm. Don't worry you'll be seeing it soon enough."

"Okay," he said with a rye attitude. Crane slid his hands in front of himself, resting them on the elevator doors.

"Don't shoot unless you're sure you won't miss." Mr. Crane advised the masked thief.

"You don't worry yourself about me, mister, I'll shoot you. No question."

"Confidence is a trait wasted on the incompetent."

"You should know, you're the one with the gun pointed at your head."

"It's not the pointing so much as the arrogance I have to listen to. You think because you have a gun, you're on top of the situation. Let me give you some free advice. You're not on top of this."

"Oh yeah?" The gunman asked.

"Oh Yeah…." Replied Mr. Crane, then he spun around, and blocked the thief's gun hand. Crane drew his backup piece and fired twenty times into the masked thief, having to reload his 9mm twice. It never hurts to be sure."

"The elevator doors opened with a light bell ring then Crane wiped the sweat from his brow and marched through the lobby, leaving one rich big shot crying to himself and one amateur lying in the bloody lift.

"What the hell?" Said the guard, fresh from his lazy nap and totally unaware of the bloodbath that had just transpired. Crane passed through the revolving doors and was back outside. He pressed the small black box in his left hand and his car was brought around to him.

"Where to sir?" The chauffeur asked as Mr. Crane got into the black Cadillac.

"How about a quiet night spot with plenty of hens and no other roosters."

"I have the perfect place, perfect that is, for a man with a fat wallet." Mr. Crane showed him the gangster roll of thousand dollar bills and they were off. The bright taillights of that luxury sedan followed them into the dark. From the back of that car, he had already started planning the next hit, the next job. It was always a challenge, whether it was guns or girls."

Jacob sat there fixed on the story, his mind filled with Mr. Crane and his suave killing. They went back to their jobs, still hearing the trumpeted notes and the strong drumbeats from down the street; then Jacob saw a gorgeous woman with dazzling green eyes waiting for a drink. The lighting of her cigarette was his cue to speed up. He stepped over to the table and asked for her drink order. She wanted a mineral water with lemon, since she was underage. He shook the blue water bottle, poured it's contents into a tall glass, and placed the fresh lemon slices on the glasses top edge. The cold tartness of it all made her scrunch up her face for a second then she smiled. The drink had been received with appreciation. He turned to walk away, averting his eyes so as not to look at her, but she stopped him.

"What happened to your face?" The kind voice asked.

"Well, a few men tried to rob me last night."

"Really. Did they hurt you bad?"

"No, It's just bruises." Pointing at his swollen eye and split lip.

"I'm glad to hear it." She said as he walked away. He had just served a woman who's beauty could steal his heart, a proposition that warmed his usually cold body.

Jacob served her for twenty-five minutes or so, then took his late evening break before the nighttime regulars got there. He read the newspaper and sipped his soda pop.

He washed off the newsprint ink and went back to working. He was in the start of waxing the bar top when he received a telegram from his dad.

Telegram: [Son. Mom is in hospital. Heart problems. Will send more news when I get it.]

Jacob ran to the back of the bar, clawing at the phone but dropped the receiver in frustration and sat on the ground. She was in trouble. The one person in this world that never stopped believing in him was in trouble and he couldn't do a damn thing to help. He shook all over; his mind was racing out of control. Jacob didn't care about his job or the apartment upstairs. All he wanted was to go home to help her. He looked to his right and picked the receiver back up. He dialed his folks' number; his dad was quiet on the other end of the line, waiting for him to say something. Then he spoke, "Listen son, I know this is a shock. Mom said you're doing good over there, so I think you shouldn't worry about coming to the hospital."

Jacob's jaw dropped. He clenched the phone and was ready to scream into it all the hateful words that came to mind. Then he thought of her, doing better and in safekeeping. He wouldn't be disrespectful for her, not now, not like that. He told his dad that he'd think it over and he'd let him know if he should expect him. Jacob tried to put the receiver back down on the catch but it fell off.

Chapter 19

▼

The Dead Line

The beeping of the dead line filled his ears and he sat there weeping behind the bar. Jacob remained there for a few minutes, until he heard a question from a soft voice.

"Are you okay?" He looked over in the direction of the female voice and told her what had just happened.

She didn't say a thing. He thought she was nodding, telling him she understood his pain. He couldn't be sure, choosing to stare at the floor through his weeping eyes.

Jacob lifted his weak body away from the floor and dusted his pants off. He glanced back over to the table and she was gone. There was only a cloud of cigarette smoke over the vacant table. Frank came in and Jacob told him all about the telegram and the phone call. He patted Jacob on the shoulder and said he knew how he felt. Thinking about Frank's fiancé story made Jacob believe that he truly did understand. Frank took him upstairs and gave him the rest of the day off. Jacob just lay there on the army cot crying as Frank fixed the busted door and pretended to not hear him sobbing.

Chapter 20

The Greenest Set of Eyes

Frank continued working on the door, tightening up screws and gluing the broken wood. Jacob just sat there on the cot and knew he'd need to go to see his mother in the hospital.

It was hot in the apartment, the windows were open, but still it was hot. Jacob asked Frank about work, he told him to not worry about it.

"That bar's not going anywhere. An illness in the family is a reason to take a break. You've got to, doctor's orders." Frank looked back to the door and went on with his work. Jacob lay back down for a minute then was regrettably reminded of his summers on the farm.

The summers would get that hot, the humidity making it hell to just breathe. He'd lie down on the wood floor of his room and would think of being someplace far away. In some quiet fantasy spot, he could write about anything that he wanted, he would be kept cool by air-conditioned surroundings. He'd get up and get a snack or watch TV, whatever he wanted. He didn't have to ask permission to use the truck or take a break.

He'd leave that tired body and would float past the flannel shirts and overalls. He'd drift over the barbed wire and the wooden pole fences. Jacob's imagination would coast with the wind, being in the company of Angels and migrating birds. He'd swoop and dive, leaving the mortals to run along the ground, trying to keep up with his impressive wingspan. Then the sounds of cars and trains would draw him to a sleepy little town, a quiet village where everyone knew each other.

He'd let himself down onto the main drag, eyeing the families driving by, hearing the church mass going on. Sometimes he'd appear in front of a mom and pop grocery store, and inside he'd see her. It was so real that he was sure she was out there in the real world. Waiting for her as a ghostly admirer. He'd lean against the dusty pane-glass windows and count the smiles that were on her face. She gave them away, free for all that were able to receive them. That hazelnut brown hair, those mythological curves, and the greenest set of eyes you'd ever see. He would pray silently for her to turn towards him, for to see her eyes up-close was to make him a free man. Just when he had his fill of that dreamed town, she would look right at the dusty windowpane and he'd disappear into a cloud of smoke.

He'd find himself lying on the floor of his room, cooled off and wearing a smile that he didn't deserve. He carried the idea of she around with him. No matter the time or the place, he was in her company. When he was wiping the countertop off, he imagined it was their kitchen table. If Jacob were doing dishes, he'd convince himself that she had just moments ago, held the very glass that he now washed.

Jacob could smell her perfume on everything, it permeated him through and through.

"You done day dreaming?" Frank shouted, snapping him out of his trance.

"I wasn't day dreaming." Jacob shouted back.

"Like hell you weren't. Now come over here and help me move these tables." So he did as he was told, jumbling up the chairs and tables to the far corner of the bar in order to let Frank plan out a new seating arrangement.

"Wouldn't it be easier to just do the new plan, then move the stuff around?"

"No, Mr. Writer, it wouldn't."

"Okay Mr. Crane." Jacob retorted.

"Don't ever call me that!" Frank screamed at him, dropping his end of the table that they were moving and staring angrily at Jacob.

"I'm sorry, Frank. I didn't mean anything by it. I just thought…scratch that. I didn't think." Frank paced back and forth, keeping Jacob in his sights the whole time. He was breathing heavy through his nose; nostrils expanded like a bull. He wiped his forehead and looked out the front window.

"Oh, look, let's take a fifteen minute break and cool off. I don't know what I was thinking, moving all this stuff around on the hottest damn day of the year."

"Okay Frank. No problem." Frank wiped the saliva from his chin and blew his nose. He was tense, and his body showed it. He was on his way to a cold drink.

Frank made up another "Nothing Special," while Jacob swept up the floor where the newly moved tables and chairs were.

"Put that down and come have a drink."

"I am, I just want to get this dirt cleaned up. Since all the chairs are moved and all."

"Fine, but don't take too long, you're still gonna have a drink."

"I promise." Frank let him go on working and he kept on pouring. The final dustpan worth of chore was dumped out and Jacob was on his way to healing a parched throat. He stepped up to the bar-rail and ordered a sarsaparilla in his best John Wayne voice. This made Frank crack up, letting some of the 'Nothing Special' leak out of his grinning mouth.

"Damn boy! You should do a comedy hour with an accent like that!"

"Thanks, but I think I'll find something I'm more qualified for."

"Good luck youngster." He went back to drinking a little more. Jacob reached over to his newly poured 'Nothing Special' and in a split second saw his reflection in the mirror behind the bottles. On his face was a look of slyness; an expression used by only the very immoral eyebrow raisers. He tightened his fingers around the glass and tried to forget how much work was still ahead.

Chapter 21

▼

The Bellhop

The work of the day went off well; Frank got the Big Apple's seating reorganized and Jacob swept. All morning and all afternoon, sweeping was all he did. They went through the usual stuff with customers, some wanting a colder beer, some a bubblier pop. It was like working at a daycare for babies that drink booze. The evening crept up on them, and then 1 a.m. was there.

Jacob got to make last call and he ushered everyone out after his or her drink was done. He locked up and sat at the counter with Frank. Jacob had been bothered by thoughts of his mother's illness. Should he go? Would he even be able to? The thoughts were so abundant that they choked off his air and it was all he could do not to panic.

"Want to hear another story?" Frank's eyes telling Jacob he was eager at the prospect of telling another one.

"Sure, if you want to." He answered, thinking a story might do him some good.

"I want to." Frank said with strange enthusiasm.

"This one's about Mr. Crane, but it takes place just a few months ago."

"Let's hear it."

"I wrote it down, you mind if I read from this?" He was holding a piece of worn paper, his eyes asking Jacob to say yes.

"Go for it Frank."

Frank leaned back and held the paper to the light, "The bellhop straightened his posture and nodded forward in accordance to the sharply dressed man." Frank looked up to see if Jacob liked the beginning.

"The alligator bags hung safely on the trolley, finding their way into the elevator with Mr. Crane following. He looked around the cramped little lift, eyeing the nonchalant behavior of the porter and his yet shaking hand. The doors closed and then the floor shook with a slight sting of unseen velocity. He could feel the lift slow down, as if approaching the needed floor, but the lit up lights above showed that they were still twenty floors away. The elevator shook then came to a halt. Crane steadied himself, arms reaching out to the mirrored walls and to the swinging bags. The bellhop caught a grip on the handrail and spun his head around. He looked different, the arrogant smile from the lobby was gone, and in it's place there was a look of seriousness Mr. Crane had known well."

"The bellhop reached his hand into his inner-pocket and retrieved a small pistol with an attached silencer. Mr. Crane wasn't surprised, and so, by the time the weapon was pulled, the amateur assassin dropped to the floor. Mr. Crane had executed the movement perfectly, the amateur's throat had been crushed and not a bruise on him. Crane picked up the pistol and placed it in the elevator's ashtray. The doors finally opened and he stepped out. No one was in the hallway; no one seemed to be waiting for him. He grabbed his bags off the cart and walked over to the room. Room 234, bought and paid for by his handler. Not 239 that he had rented that busy evening. Mr. Crane couldn't afford to relax for even an instant, so used to behaving in a cloak and dagger manner. He tossed his suit coat on the bed and nudged the bags into the room. He took another look around, then went inside. Double locking the door and even disabling the electronic key-card system, Crane made his temporary digs as cozy as possible. If he wanted fresh towels or his bed turned down, he'd just as soon do it himself.

He locked the windows and kept the TV set off. He opened the suitcase, which was made out of a bulletproof material and checked his assorted goodies. Everything was where it was supposed to be, not a piece was out of place.

He closed his portable arsenal and packed it safely under the bed. The .45 he carried under his jacket even came out, choosing to leave it resting on the hutch. He peered outside of the high-story window and took in enough of the scenic skylight. He'd had his fill of flashing lights and neon promises, he was ready for bed, but the bed just wasn't ready for him.

The cold shower was desperately needed; causing goosebumps to rise then fall, the toweling warmed him afterward. He wiped the beaded water from his washed face, deciding at that moment that he'd need a shave tomorrow. He styled his dark hair with the water from the shower, letting it dampen the T-shirt and his shorts, which he was now about to sleep in. He trudged off the sopping wet bathroom mat and into the carpeted room; checking the door again, looking through the peephole for unexpected company. Apparently, tonight was going to be uneventful.

The cold hotel sheets felt heavenly, reducing his tough-guy facade to that of a crossing guard. He tucked himself in and flicked on the TV, watching the dancing figures as his chest rose and fell. He could feel his tired eyelids, getting heavier and heavier. He clicked off the set and began to fall asleep, his hand checking the loaded .45 under his pillow and then he drifted off.

He was never much for alarm clocks, so he always had a wake-up call. There was just something so 'morning after' in hearing a beautiful woman's voice at 6 a.m., even if she hadn't spend the night. He stretched up his numb arms and let out a sound that was somewhere between a primal scream and the sound a person makes after farting in a public place. Either way, Mr. Crane was ready to start the day. He walked over to the propped up suitcase and pulled from it a pair of socks, a black T-shirt, his belt, and some other essentials.

He yawned a few times, walking into the fresh bathroom and onto the cool morning tile. He set the clothes down on the sinks counter, turning to pick up a copy of Esquire magazine. His tense legs hopped over to the bathmat that was, to his surprise, dry and quite warm. He dragged it with his feet over to the toilet, then took his seat for the morning ritual of all men. The toilet seat was chilly, but at least his feet were warm.

The recently relieved gentleman went through the typical routine, from hair to clothes, finishing up with re-loading and cleaning his two .45's. He put the specially crafted pistols into their holsters, waiting for the sound of their magnetic snaps. He had installed magnets into the holsters, so that the force of him grabbing them would cause them to release, but if he were to bend down, they wouldn't budge.

He picked up the phone and told the operator his room number and that he had luggage to go down. After putting the phone down, Mr. Crane used the time before the next bellhop would be there to wipe down the room for fingerprints. There wasn't much to clean up, having spent the night primarily in latex gloves. Next he took the sheets and pillowcases from the bed and stuffed them into a garbage bag in his suitcase. He'd take them with him, to be destroyed later. No use in simply wiping the bed clean. DNA and all that.

The porter arrived as expected; not paying attention to the missing sheets, hoping for a big tip. They got into the elevator and waited for the lobby. Halfway down, he turned to Mr. Crane and asked, 'did you hear about the murder yesterday?' Crane looked at him with a tourist's eye, as if he was filled with disbelief.

"Yeah, some guy in a bellhop's outfit got killed on the elevator. He even had a gun with him, probably drugs." Mr. Crane nodded his head with true suburbia interest.

"I'm sure glad it wasn't on my shift." He mumbled, trying to hide the fear he felt.

"Well, you live by the sword…" the elevator doors opened, interrupting Mr. Crane's proverb, giving him an excuse to drop the topic.

"Have a good day sir," the bellhop said to the well-dressed man, obviously waiting for a dip.

"Same to you, young man," Crane slipped a c-note into the his hand.

His black suit, his black shoes, the black shirt and the black tie; they all made him the mysterious man he felt he was. Probably the only professional killer that on occasion, wanted all eyes in the room firmly fixed on him. He stepped up to the counter, pulling his billfold from his inner coat pocket, "I'd like to check out now please." He said to the pretty girl tending to the front desk.

"Yes sir, just one moment." She had to lean down behind the counter, then came up with a stack of paper and a flushed face. As her smiling face returned to its original color, she slid a form over to him, a survey for the service he received. He told her he'd fill it out later and drop it in the mail. That was good enough for her, because in 3 minutes, his bill was paid and he was walking out the door. Mr. Crane had a car waiting for him, his bags were already in the trunk."

Chapter 22

▼

Mr. Nova and the Motown Honey

"It's good to see you again sir, it's been too long." The driver said as Crane sat down in the backseat.

"I want to thank you again for what you did, it was really...."

"It's nothing Manny, just forget it." Mr. Crane looked him right in the eyes; he knew to shut up, to just drive the car. There's nothing Crane hated more than gratitude. So he found and killed the men that raped Manny's sister. He'd just rather go on with his life.

The car left the hotel and they were off to an office building. I can't give specifics, but it was a hell of a big building. He knew that the weather was going to be bone chilling, but what do you expect from Detroit in the winter? They sped down the highway, Mr. Crane's nerves totally calm. Yet, if you were to put an amateur in the same position, vomiting would be the only sound of the trip. Instead, he had Manny put some real music on, Motown honey as he called it. Soulful Ms. Aretha lulled him into a peaceful, yet dangerous calm. He told Manny to turn it off and while he was at it, to open the front windows. Specks of snow flew into the car, but Manny didn't say a thing. He just quietly shivered as he drove Crane to his next job.

He had Manny leave with his gear; having to check out the security for the building first. Mr. Crane walked into the lobby with a map and a pair of wide rimmed glasses on. The guards jumped on the chance to escort him out, although he tried to convince them he was just lost. He counted two guards at the desk, two at the elevator doors, and one sitting in a far corner; his seat surrounded by magazines and candybar wrappers. He'd shoot the slob first, the two at the desks, then the elevator duo. That is five bullets total but he'd spend two on each of them to be sure. Now that he was back outside, Crane looked up, the east face of the skyscraper gently reflected the morning sun, allowing him to see nothing about it's interior."

"The mounted cameras watched as he left their property. He realized there must be more than the five guards he had counted in the lobby. There was no monitoring equipment where they were, so a back up team was more than likely.

Manny picked him up at the rendezvous site, a busy bus station with a drunken guy and a mother with her two kids. She was saying to the kids to be good at school, to do as the teacher said. She reached into her purse for their lunch money, but came up with only some breath spray and a useless gas card. Mr. Crane pulled out a folded C-note and dropped it on the ground right behind them.

"Excuse me ma'am, I think you dropped something." He pointed behind her; she looked up and smiled. Mr. Crane saw a tear, right before she winked at him and mouthed the words, 'thank you." He nodded, and with a flick of his hand, Manny pulled to the broken cement curb and he stepped into the warm black Cadillac.

Mr. Crane had noticed after getting into the car that Manny was eating something yet trying not to be seen doing so.

"Hey Manny, don't worry about it. I ate before you picked me up, so just eat your breakfast." Manny shook his head letting him know he heard. He raised the hot-dog to his mouth and they were back on their way."

"He had Manny pull into a car wash, which was a little out of the way site that an old acquaintance of his owned. They paid like everyone else, but in the middle of the wash, the floor opened up and the Cadillac was slowly lowered into a subterranean stronghold. He told Manny to stay put, Manny seemed not to mind. Mr. Crane pulled the door release, stepping out into the cold air. He lifted his arms, showing he had no weapons…knowing they'd never check his inner thigh.

He walked down a roughly lit hallway, positioned in the middle of an abandoned car-parking structure. There were streams of water running down the walls, trickling from the car wash's pipes. Mr. Crane looked around, counting and mentally marking his possible targets. Eleven against one. Those odds seem fair. He kept walking, up to the desk of a very fat man, Mr. Nova, who was the crime boss of Detroit. He took off his over-coat and sat down opposite Mr. Nova. They call him that, because he was only able to ride around in a gutted out Nova. Hell, that's just the way nicknames go.

"So you're gonna pay me a visit…back in De-toilet, for work no doubt."

"Don't worry Mr. Nova, you're still on my good-graces." Crane said to him with a sarcastic tone.

"That's good to hear, you wanna canoli?" He pointed his chubby finger over to a carton of the pastries.

"Nah. I'm watching my weight." He replied while looking at Mr. Nova's struggling belt.

"So whatcha need? Guns? Bombs? Girls?"

"Not this time, just your permission to work for the next couple of days."

"Just a couple of days? It's not on any of my boys?" He asked, fumbling with a handkerchief.

"That depends on who your boys are?" Mr. Crane sneered with his hands folded in front of him.

Mr. Nova kept looking at Mr. Crane's hands, relaxing nothing on that fat body. "As long as it ain't me, you're welcome to stay." Crane tilted forward in the chair, staring Mr. Nova in the eyes, wishing he had a picture of his nervous expression, because no one would have believed him. The terror in that usually calm face was worth the trip to the Motor City.

"Since we've concluded business, I'll be going." Mr. Crane stood up, feeling a cool draft against his neck, predicting a punch already thrown. He dropped down, punched the wise guy in the nuts, grabbed his right hand, and bent it 90 degrees the wrong way. The wise guys' echoes of pain filled the underground structure, the screams quite deafening.

"Damn your fast! You never relax, do you?" Mr. Nova asked through his laughter.

"Never," he said, not even winded. "I'll be seeing you."

"Not if I see you first." Mr. Nova quipped back to him. Crane went back the way he came, eyeing the pissed off stares of those dangerous men in the hall. Each one of them wanted to kill him, to be the man who popped 'Mr. Crane.'

"I'd like to see you mooks try it." He yelled to the men standing between him and the Cadillac.

"Maybe next time," answered a voice from the crowd.

"Maybe." He had his over-coat in his hands and stepped back into the car.

"Manny get us out of here." He ordered with both guns drawn behind the darkened glass.

"Sure thing Mr. Crane." Manny replied. He didn't ask what happened. Manny just did as he was told. They returned to the land of the living, the bright light of day temporarily blinding them as they exited."

Jacob could see why Mr. Crane was so feared, why he'd be so good at what he does.

"How can he kill so easily?" Jacob asked.

"I think he's just cold-blooded. If you don't have family to care about you, then what's the reward in being good?"

"I think I see what you mean." That said, Jacob was off to bed. Hopefully he would sleep, but most likely, he'd worry over his mother.

He slept well that night, envisioning his dream girl who was wearing a gold necklace with a locket attached. In the dream, he opened the locket and inside was three letters, 'KBG.' He woke up confused, not knowing if those were her initials or just random images in a tired young mind. He lay there thinking it over, then finally he got the urge to get up after hearing Frank opening the Big Apple downstairs. He wiped away the sleep from his eyes and yawned. He let the stinky air out with full lungs and yawned again. Jacob stood up from the Army cot and watched the sun slowly rising outside of his window. He itched his balls, pushing aside the boxers just like he'd seen in a movie somewhere.

The morning coffee wasn't brewed and breakfast was never made. This wasn't a home, like where his mother and father lived. It was just a room that he slept in.

He started sobbing and crying, stomping on the tile with his barefeet, embarrassed to be so vulnerable to his feelings. 'What if I freak out at work?' He began obsessing, seeing the moment too clearly. He laid out the situation and replayed its humiliation over and over again. Jacob grabbed his head and held it firmly. He needed to steady the spinning sensation, taking control of the speedily crazy moment.

Jacob came out of the thought carousel, dizzy and a little nauseous. Coffee and breakfast sounded unusually good, weirdly appealing to a guy that never ate before noon. He used a dirty T-shirt that was lying on the floor to clean his sweaty face off, then realized it was the shirt he'd planned to wear that day, being the only shirt in his select wardrobe that wasn't permanently stained.

Chapter 23

The Cromwell Diner

He put it on anyway, not minding the yellowish swipe that went across its front. The collar was untouched, and that was all he cared about. He slipped a pair of socks on then his brown leather shoes. His Uncle Mike Bradley gave those shoes to him. Jacob never thought he'd keep them after leaving home, but he just didn't have it in him to break in a new pair.

The now repaired door slammed shut, followed by his heavy footsteps as he ran down the stairs. He clenched the end of the railing and spun himself around to the entrance of the bar. Jacob grabbed the glass door and looked through the etchings, just in time to see Frank counting last night's earnings. He opened the door and walked in.

"Need some help?" Jacob jokingly asked.

"Sure come on over." Frank answered, raising the butcher knife up.

"On second thought..." Frank nodded and Jacob stayed near the bar. Frank was funny that way, like a dog guarding his bowl to a fault. He would bite at you even if you were reaching down to help him.

Jacob kept yawning for most of the morning, not serving a single drop of booze until noon. However, when 12 came around, all the regulars suddenly appeared. He glanced over at the darkened booth and thought maybe one day. One day he'd see what all the fuss was about with Mr. Crane. He laughed to himself and continued with another workday. Frank was his usual pleasant self, telling dirty jokes about horny priests to his own 'congregation' of listeners. Some people laughed, some people pretended to laugh, others just sat quietly until the subject of the conversation changed to something they could joke about.

"Hey kid, what time's it?" Frank said to him, as he sat surrounded by the lushes and drunks.

"It's about 6 p.m."

"Then call it a night and go and find yourself something fun to do."

"I can't Frank, I need to work to pay for my ticket home. My mom is sick, remember?"

"I remember, I remember…" His voice was trailing off as he reached into his inner vest pocket and pulled out a plane ticket.

"Leaves in three days, at 9:30 a.m. sharp! If you're not on it I'll bust your ass."

"But how? I can't. I just can't. Thanks anyway Frank but…"

"Damn it boy are you dumb or something? You needed a ticket, now you have a ticket. Don't be so damned uptight!"

"You sure about this?"

"Get!" He stood up as if he was on his way to make good on his ass busting promise.

Jacob ran out of the bar, ending in the street, tucking his plane ticket for home into his breast pocket. He needed to figure some things out. The cars whizzed by, the exhaust gathering at his level, taking its time to fade out. He kept running until he got to the Cromwell Diner.

This beautiful woman, who amazingly didn't frown on dirty, scruffy men, owned it. She would wait for them to stop sweating from the hot sun, which they just escaped from, and then she would come over to the table and let them speak their piece. About lunch that is.

She would do this delicious turn as she wrote down the last of the table's orders, and would gracefully stroll back to the kitchen. Jacob would sit there, waiting for her to walk back out of the steamy room, and it was then that she would give him a wink. He didn't have to order dessert; he got something sweeter for free.

She never laid a hand on him, but every look was Heaven. Sometimes, if the diner wasn't too busy, she would sit down with him and they'd talk. About the weather at first, but as they got to know each other, it became more personal. She told him about how she was picked on in school, how the other girls didn't like her because of the run-down trailer that she had to live in. Strangely, Jacob was glad she was poor as a kid, that she earned compassion instead of popularity. He told her his own sob stories, about Bishop Springs and all the areas of his life that weren't turning out the way he had hoped. He told her how his mom, before he made up his mind to leave home, told him to forgive his father, that he was a different man before the money incident. She told him stories that made Jacob want to believe in him again. Like clockwork, Doyle would act like a selfish bastard and ruin the moment. Emily would see the respect fade from his dim eyes, wanting him to understand something she didn't even believe in. She tried to console Jacob, telling him that he was his own man and didn't have to be like his father if he didn't want to.

Jacob told her about how he didn't go out with friends, or with anyone his own age. He just couldn't relate to them, he was far too serious of a person. She understood what he meant by "too serious" because she too had noticed it about him. His face was always posed in a severe, focused look. She felt bad for him and for all the fun he was missing.

Tracy Cromwell listened to Jacob's stories, though they all seemed to end with the last sentences from the paragraph above. She'd giggle then go back to work, always ending their talks with putting a free piece of lemon pie in front of him. He'd thank her, and she would go over to another table to tend to their orders. She never treated him like other people, never making him believe he was obligated. That appealed to him, even more than that candy-coated sway.

He ate the pie, not letting the meringue stick to his fork or the tart lemon pucker his lips. He put the tip on the table and wished it were more. Jacob heard the sound of someone getting smokes out of the cigarette machine, then the door shut. He looked upwards, seeing a gray sky and a shy sun. There was a violent wind starting to build and the pedestrians doing their shopping darted into shops they really didn't want to visit, just to escape the wind. Looking out on that dismal day, he wanted that oppressively hot sun back above him. However, it was stubbornly hiding so he left the day to its own affairs.

He ran through the deserted alleyways and unkempt side streets, jumping over garbage cans and dodging requests from the homeless. He wanted to give them some money, but he was about ten bucks away from joining them.

He was heading over to Jilly's for a visit. He had seen her off and on but both were busy with work. She would come into the Big Apple with her friends and he'd serve them. Jilly would try to talk to him about how his week was going but he always had other customers or Frank needed his help.

He knocked on her door and then went around to the backdoor. No one was home so he hauled ass back to the bar.

Jacob knew his way around Arcadia, finding all the best shortcuts and unknown paths. He loved to run through people's backyards, then he'd hurdle their fences as he escaped into the next yard. He wore his leather shoes on those days, since they were lighter than the heavy combat boots he had bought from the Salvation Army Resale Store in Manistee.

It was now a full rainstorm and Jacob was happy to be back to the Big Apple. Frank saw him standing outside the entrance, stomping off the mud on his shoes that had collected while he ran through the backyards in between Jilly's and the bar. The rain was falling straight down, pouring onto the street, and darkening the sky.

"Getting wet out there?" Frank asked as he walked in soaked.

"No Frank, I like to take showers with my clothes on."

"To each his own." He chimed back not giving Jacob's sarcasm a second thought. Jacob asked him if he needed him for the next ten minutes, Frank shook his head 'no.'

Chapter 24

The Broken Doorknob

Jacob stepped again into the cool mist and hard flung droplets, racing to the steps, then up to his door, only then, realizing his keys were in his jacket back in the bar.

Therefore, he ran back down the steps, into the bar, slid across the floor with his muddy shoes, provoking Frank to start yelling, then back outside and up to the apartment door. The doorknob was broken and he had to jiggle it just right to get it to open. He hurried into the one-room abode and stripped down to his nakedness. His hair and shirt were soaked, making a puddle on the floor near the front door, where they were tossed. Jacob walked around the room, totally relaxed that no one was on the street in such a storm. He opened the windows and the curtains. He even went so far as to sit on the windowsill and watched the rain pour. That ended when a lumber truck came barreling down M-22, nearly scaring him to death and almost causing him to fall out of the window. Bare-assed naked and bruised, he would have looked the part of village idiot to all the merchants and customers drinking in the bar downstairs.

Jacob went back to the army cot and let himself air dry. The weather outside was overcast as it rained. He liked that type of day, because he had an excuse to not be outside doing some thing just for the sake of working outside. Too few could appreciate a day like that, especially those of Jacob's age. He felt like a lazy old man with a pocket full of money. He dozed off, feeling the familiar comfort of days long gone, gently drifting in and out of his fanciful mind.

He was feeling sorry for himself, reminded of everything he didn't have. He wanted to know what a woman's lips felt like as they were pressed against his. He wanted to experience the freedom of dining out and not worrying about the money he had just spent on a meal. He was tired of ordering the cheapest thing on the menu just because he was close to broke. It stung him in his mind to think of all the rude, hateful people that had wealth and did not have to do a damn thing for it. They have no conscience, he thought. They're just here to make things tough for us good people. Jacob wasn't so sure he was one of the good people. Besides, what did anyone get for being good? "Being taken advantage of," was his answer.

Deciding that cynical thinking really wasn't going to solve anything, Jacob turned his attention to playing a game in his head. This game involved him fantasizing about adventures and being a hero. First, he would think about what he would have to do, whom he'd have to save. Then he'd imagine the environment and how the witnesses in his fantasy would react to his heroism. He loved this game and did it whenever he was too geeked up to sleep. He slipped deep into it, describing for himself the clothes and atmosphere of a daring house fire rescue. He could practically smell the paint on the walls burning, the choking smoke, and scorching heat that would accumulate above 4 feet high. He planned how he would get through the flame-licked hallways, then into the bedrooms to save the children trapped in the house. Then in a dramatic escape, he would tie the bed-sheets together and would lower the kids to the ground unharmed.

The ending was always tricky because he had two options: one, he imagines the 'martyr' scenario, where he saves the kids and smiles at them, just as the house blows up. Then there was the second scenario, where he would save the kids then he would disappear back into the house. Later, the police would search the remains of the house, but would not find his body. 'Maybe he was an angel,' the neighbors would say. This always made him smile.

It was because of this whimsical feeling, this intoxicating sense of false achievement, that he didn't think anything of the young woman standing at his doorstep. Apparently, she knocked a little harder than his door could take, getting a sudden view of his sprawled naked body on that musty army cot.

"Oh I'm so sorry!" She squeaked, covering her eyes, then diverting her head, although she was being soaked from the rainstorm as she stood looking in from his raining landing.

"No, please…come in." He grabbed a pile of newspapers and held them in front and back of himself.

"Frank said I could find you here. If this is a bad time…" She started to turn for the door.

"Actually this is a perfect time." Though he had no idea of what she wanted.

"Well, okay." She put her hand down and saw him standing there, newsprint pressed against his privates. "You must be a big fan of that writer." Pointing to the column that covered, well, his column.

"I find it rather short, but distinguished." She laughed, so he knew it was all right for him to relax.

"Here, I'll put some clothes on and we'll go down to the bar."

"That sounds great." Jacob was eager to leave his apartment; scared she'd look around his place and think less of him.

Now that he was fully dressed and ready for whatever, they made their way to a well-lit booth in the bar and had a few sodas.

"You go into Tracy Cromwell's Diner don't you?"

"Yeah, about three times a week at least."

"I know you from somewhere else, don't I?"

"I'm not sure. I work in here." Her face lit up and Jacob could tell she remembered him.

"Your mother has been ill. I was the girl you served before you received the news." She did look familiar, but he really wasn't convinced that was where he knew her.

"Do you mind if I take my contacts out? They're driving me nuckin futs!" Jacob laughed loudly at her jumbled comment as she removed her brown colored contacts. She put them away, then returned her gaze to him.

"I see you there from time to time, but you usually leave so fast I never got to ask you something. Do you have plans for tonight? I mean, I wanted to ask you out."

"Oh." He was speechless, it was the first time he'd ever been asked out. It was also a moment of great revelation for him, because he looked across that table right into the green eyes of his hallucination temptress. Jacob remembered her face, her delicate beauty so vividly, his mind reeling with excitement. So this was how it felt, he thought to himself. Love. He was panicking a little bit, but curious to get to know such a gorgeous girl.

"I'd love to go out with you." Trying not to sound too over zealous, but failing miserably. First Jacob had to ask Frank for the night off. All it took was one glimpse at Mia. Frank ordered Jacob to have the night off. Jacob came over to Mia and told her he could take her out, but he'd need to go upstairs to get something.

"Great." She said, seeing him leave the bar and then heard his footsteps going up to his apartment. She couldn't see him rushing over to his closet and pulling out an envelope that contained his life savings. He shoved the money into his pocket and ran back down the stairs. She heard him coming back down so she met him at the door.

"Lead the way my lady," he said bowing down with a touch of Victorian etiquette. Mia allowed him to kiss the top of her hand, letting Jacob get a slight sample of her warmth.

"Your hands are so cold, do you want a jacket?" She was looking at his thin, cold hands.

"No, it's just the way my body is. I can't even feel it." They were walking out to through the parking lot. The rain had stopped; right there, Jacob was sure it had stopped just for the two of them.

Chapter 25

The First Date

He felt like the luckiest man in Arcadia, not knowing what the future would hold. Holding such a beautiful woman's hand made him smile widely, knowing that jealous men were staring as they walked by.

They strolled down the sidewalks, around mud puddles, and under store canopies that were still dripping with warm water. Eventually, they arrived at the Arcadian Crest Hotel, which had a very well known restaurant. Jacob had been saving his money for a new typewriter, but he didn't think twice about spending it that night.

The host of the restaurant escorted the cute couple into the beautifully lit dining room. There were chandeliers hanging above, all adorned with curved light fixtures. Their table was near the far wall, set away from the chattering voices that were in the main section of the room. Jacob took her jacket and his, handing them to the waiter, who then gave them to the coat room attendant. Jacob pulled her chair out for her, then scooted her up to the table. She was brushing aside her silky bangs, peering around the room at other people's food. The waiter came back once Jacob was seated;

offering menus and taking drink orders. They ordered a bottle of wine, but they were carded, so they changed it to Iced Tea.

The embarrassment over being underage quickly left them and they flipped through the tall canvas menus. The tassels hooked to the outer binding tickled her hands, causing her to think it was a spider. Mia dropped the menu onto the table, knocking over the water glasses. The tablecloth was soaked so the waiter hurried over and grabbed the cloth's four corners, lifted the wet mess off of the table, then two other men rushed over and placed a fresh set of tableware down. Mia and Jacob were dazzled by such excellent service.

"Wasn't that cool?" Mia asked.

"It was definitely cool." Jacob was getting nervous. His voice deepened and he asked her, "have you ever eaten here?"

"Yes, I have. I came here last week with my parents."

"Oh I'm sorry, I wanted to take you someplace special."

"This has been very special. I think it's wonderful that you even care about making such an impromptu date so much fun." Her legs were crossed below the table; her right leg was bopping up and down against her left leg. She tapped her right pinkie fingernail tip against her teeth, as if she were considering something.

Jacob was extremely aroused by this and when she said it would be fun to dance before ordering dinner, he abruptly disagreed. He needed a few minutes to just sit there thinking about baseball or some other extinguishing thought. She said okay.

The waiter returned to them a few minutes later. He had been wearing a black penguin suit with white cummerbund before he left for their drinks, but now the cummerbund was nowhere in sight. From the gravy stains on his sleeves, they could tell that it had been a long night already and they didn't see any reason to joke with him.

"Are you ready to order?" Jacob was about to say yes, but Mia spoke up first.

"Yes, we will have the filet mignon and the salmon with raspberry sauce."

"And would you like anything else to drink?"

"I don't know," she turned to Jacob, "want anything else?"

"No, I'm good, unless you want something." She shook her head 'no.'

"Very good, you're order will be ready in a few minutes." He tucked the menus under his arm and walked to the kitchen.

"He was pretty polite, don't you think?" Mia asked.

"I think so. He looked like he could use a break."

"Everyone in here does."

"Everyone but you, green eyes." She blushed and he grinned from causing it.

They past the time before eating, talking about Arcadia, their lives, and jokes about sex. It wasn't a vulgar or inappropriate exchange; they were just flirting out of their territory. Neither had honestly been experienced in the ways of love and they fought off that insecurity by showing a sexed up bravado.

Mia had taken off her sandals and was rubbing her feet against Jacob's legs. His ears grew beet red, then he began sweating. She was laughing out loud as he took a few large gulps of the ice water and attempted to compose himself. She thought he was going to have a heart attack from it, so she slipped her sandals back on and sat up straight.

He unbuttoned his collar and let the heat from his chest vent out. He had stopped sweating but his mouth was dry. He couldn't remember ever being that excited. Their food arrived, so as Mia put her fork to good use, Jacob excused himself to go to the restroom. Mia acknowledged his leaving by waving her fork as she chewed a mouthful of the steak.

He squeezed through the now tightly packed dining room, making his way to the kitchen. Once out of her sight, he ran over to the waiter who was waiting near the kitchen for another table's order.

"Hey, I need you to do me a favor."

"Okay, what's the favor?"

"I want you to write up the bill now and tell me the total."

"What?"

"I need to make sure that I've got enough money."

"Oh. Sure, just a second." The waiter went to the register in the back office and added up the meal. It came out to $85.36, plus tax. Jacob had $75.00. He told the waiter this and promised him that he would pay the deficit back. The waiter took his money and then reached into his tip jar. He counted out the rest of the bill and looked at Jacob as if to tell him 'I'm doing you a big favor. Don't screw me over.' "What time do you open here tomorrow?"

"4 p.m."

"I'll have your money then."

"I hope so." Jacob felt microscopic, having to borrow money from the waiter to pay the bill. He could have just told Mia and asked her for the rest. Yeah right! He might as well have painted 'cheap bastard' on his forehead. He returned to the table and found Mia still chewing on a piece of steak.

"How is it?" He asked.

"Magnificent," she said with her mouth full, "try some!" She stabbed a beef square with the fork and held it out over the table to him. He didn't know if he was supposed to take the fork from her or bite the steak as she held the fork. He played it safe and gestured to take the fork from her, she pulled it back and asked, "are you afraid that I've got cooties?"

"Of course I don't, it's just that I might."

"I'll take my chances." She held the steak up once more and he accepted it happily. She went back to eating, as Jacob made his plate. He wasn't really that hungry and felt stupid for spending so much on a first date. She's gonna think I'm made of money, he thought to himself.

The bus boy cleared the table, leaving their glasses of Iced Tea and their napkins. Mia rested back in her chair, lightly rubbing her stomach. She now had a puppy belly, with the soft curve starting below her navel. The dress she was wearing strangely accented it, as if she had worn it just for that effect.

"Do you want me to leave the waiter his tip?" She was going into her purse to find some bills.

"Nah, I'll just go and pay the bill. I'll have them put the tip on my credit card." He was too eager to leave the table, just to go pay the bill. She guessed that something was up but she didn't want to pry. She told him that she would wait for him there. He smiled then hurried through the dining room. As he stepped out of the room, the waiter came in through the kitchen entrance. He came to get their table ready for the next customers. Mia told him that her date was paying for the bill and his tip, just so he would know. He rolled his eyes and kept on working.

"What was that for?" She asked him.

"It's nothing. Really."

"No, what's your problem?" He leaned down and whispered, "your boyfriend owes me twenty bucks for the bill. He didn't have enough green to pay for your little night out." She didn't know what to say.

The waiter finished his work and left the room the same way that he came. Jacob came back to her holding their jackets. "All taken care of. I think I even get frequent flyer miles from using my card here." He helped slip her jacket on, then put his own on. She wasn't saying anything. She wants to go home, I know it, he thought. It's getting late, almost midnight. I cannot believe she's out on a date with a guy like me. "I think you should take me home." Jacob's heart sank.

"No problem Mia. We'll go right now."

"Jacob, it's just that I don't want to be a bother to you."

"A bother? How in the world could you think you're a bother?"

"I know about the bill for this dinner." His thin face grimaced. She touched his shoulder in order to make him relax.

"It's okay if you're not rich. I just wish you had told me the truth." She started out of the room, Jacob followed behind her. The waiter that had served him was near the kitchen door, with a thumbs up pointed at him.

"Mia? Wait for me near the hosts' desk. There's something I need to take care of."

"All right." He turned and walked forcefully to the kitchen, lining up with the waiter and his soon-to-be dropped tray.

"What did you tell her?" He grabbed the waiter by the suit coat and shoved him through the kitchen doors. The waiter slammed into one of the metal slicing tables. He dropped down to the floor, whimpering like a coward. "I told her…that…you didn't have enough money for dinner." Jacob checked the dining room for security guards. There was only the floor manager and he was headed right for the kitchen door.

"Consider this confrontation your tip." The only other way out was through the service door, which he took to get out into the back alley then ran back up front of the restaurant. He pulled the front door open and grabbed Mia's hand. They took no time to get out of the parking lot and didn't stop until they were two blocks away. By then, both were breathing heavily, but only one knew why.

"What's with the 100-yard dash?" Mia asked as she sat on a bench.

"I just thought something spontaneous would make the end of the date fun."

"Fun?"

"Yep." She looked sleepily at him; "this has been fun."

"Look Mia, I'm sorry I didn't tell you about not having money. I'm so embarrassed." He turned away from her; "you're just so beautiful that I couldn't see our first date being spent at the diner."

"I would have preferred that." Jacob took her by the hand and they walked across M-22, then inside of Tracy Cromwell's diner.

"I don't have anymore money."

"That's fine. I've got a few bucks." Her left hand retrieved a wad of folded bills, all twenty's. She didn't let Jacob see them and she zipped up her purse after shoving the money back down to its bottom.

"Dessert's on me." He grinned at the idea of dessert being on her.

"Oh stop it!" She was showing her bubbly cheerfulness with every gorgeous smile.

"On second thought, maybe we should just have pie."

The diner closed at 1 a.m., the city was starting to wind down. She was tired; her yawning tipped him off. He walked her home, under the ever-watchful stars that cascaded the cool Michigan night. The streetlamps were going off one by one, letting them see more and more of the night sky.

He waited as she went through the heavy iron gates and then he thanked her for the lovely evening. She was shivering from the cool gripping air, looking back over her shoulder at the front door of her house. She'd soon be warm, one way, or another.

"Don't you want to come in?" She asked with an inviting look.

"More than anything, but not tonight."

"You're so cute. By the way, what's your lastname? You didn't say all evening."

"James, but you can just call me whatever you want," he said backing out of the mansions' yard.

"What can I call you? Is it too early in our relationship for pet names?" He asked, turning the focus onto her.

"Mia Sullivan. Or just Mia…my sweet." She had no idea of how sugary the sound of her name was. He had a wide smile on his wide-awake face, which she took joy in seeing. With a wave to her, he backed away from the temptation, disappeared behind the stone wall, and ran joyfully down the darkened street.

"Mia, Mia, Mia, Mia, Mia." Jacob whispered, then stated, then sung, then screamed, then announced to the world. He had been hit by an off-shot arrow of Cupid, struck straight in the heart. He danced like a fool, like a man who's just received a taste of summer after a lifetime of winter.

He enjoyed the way it felt, then hoped she felt the same. Her words were so sweet, so poetic. He grinned and laughed, even as couples walked by, trying not to get involved with this love-blessed mad man. He climbed lightpoles and hopped over benches. His lungs couldn't get enough air, for the air, at sometime, had been Mia's. She had breathed it once; it had been with her in an intimate nature. He grew jealous of the air, wanting to know if it truly appreciated being so close to her.

He smiled and giggled, chuckled and danced, he loved life again, and its ironic romance. Life was ironic because he met Mia when he was metaphorically and literally, naked. She saw all that he was, and she still wanted him. That made him stop dancing and prancing. He leaned against the lightpole and began to weep the happy tears of a man who's come to the end of a quest for love. He had survived the worry over his mother's heart problems only days before, and now he was being rewarded with Mia's love.

He was weeping and dancing, sobbing and prancing. The rhythm that he carried with him would have made Fred Astaire envious, every beat and tap of his foot perfectly timed and in place. Jacob now had a plane ticket to go home, he danced and danced, knowing the day would take care of him. It had watched over him wonderfully up to that point.

He flew up the steps to his apartment, never once touching the mossy steps. The door opened for him, no hassle with jiggling the doorknob that night. He floated into bed, instantly ready for a long sleep. He looked back out of the window and saw the glare of the city lights. It continued to lightly rain, the droplets on the window gave the lights outside an otherworldly glow, shining kindly for his bedtime pleasure.

Chapter 26

No Ordinary Morning

Jacob had gone to bed with peaceful intentions, eager to imagine. As the clouds and sparkling lights of his dream gave way, there was only one face he could see. It was Mia. He was standing in a lush garden, surrounded on all sides with apple-blossoms and singing birds. It was paradise according to Jacob.

Mia stood near a pond, wearing a flowing purple gown, her hair naturally free to blow in the gentle breeze of his subconscious. She was picturesque. He accidentally turned his head, seeing a shadow as it crept through the bushes. Its cold darkness withered the plants as it passed over. The leaves on nearby trees were caught by a powerful gust that surprised him, carrying the green patches upwards.

The shadow approached Mia, Jacob tried with all his soul to warn her, struggling to scream but he couldn't. His legs were immobilized, rooted in the gardens' lawn. Mia merely smiled as she was unknowingly preyed upon by the mysterious dark. He tried to get to her, to protect her, but it was futile. The black mass that he had dreaded reared up as if to stand like a man and with its claws curved and extended, it picked Mia up. She screamed and cried for Jacob, but he was motionless. His fear welcomed him back to reality, leaving him covered in cold, terror-induced sweat.

He sat up in the bed, looking around the room, making sure it had all been a self-deception. He lay back, uncomfortable in the chilly, wet sheets. He shivered a bit, then closed his eyes.

This time his sleeping dropped him off on a park bench, watching nude senior citizens as they ran by. He laughed at the insanity of it all, though, it made perfect sense to him. It was the same sort of familiarity that people experience when they recognize a face, but can't place where they know it from. Jacob sat on the bench and he tried not to focus on the jiggly skin and the wrinkled butts.

A while after the naked grannies finished their impromptu parade, a fat little cherub with two feathery wings came down from the sky and sat on his lap. In the angels' hands, held protectively to its chest, was a machine gun. The giggling angel turned to look him straight in the eyes and handed the gun to Jacob.

"What's this for?" Jacob asked.

"It's nothing personal, I just thought you could use it."

"Use it for what?" The angel pointed a chubby finger at the crowd of old people who were now dressed with bull's eyes on their backs. The angel smiled and said, "Go with God." Jacob woke immediately; his hands propped up as if he were still holding the weapon. "Go with God?" He asked himself with a joking laugh. By the light of that early morning he got up from his army cot and began to get ready for work. He had a silly attitude, joking and talking to himself about the night full of unbelievable images. He shut the apartment door as best as it could be and walked down the apartment stairs. In fact, he didn't walk; he floated, merely going through the motions of touching the ground in order to not draw any undue attention.

Frank welcomed him with open arms, though they were stretched open because of the box he was carrying. He offered to help but Frank insisted he was fine. Jacob even offered to sweep up for him, moments after he dropped the box. Again, Jacob received a smile and a firm "no."

He delighted in the day so much, that he asked Frank for permission to do the Big Apple's errands about town. Frank was happy to hand over the chores. Jacob wanted to help him, but moreover, he wanted to see Mia.

The walk over to her house, just a few minutes after taking care of the Apple's errands, was brief. He was three houses away when he found a group of children huddled over a butterfly. Its wing had been broken but Jacob thought he could help. They watched as he picked it up and then lifted it, as to toss it to fly. It did not leave his palm so he tried again. It stayed, clutching to his skin.

"Hey mister, is it gonna be okay?" One of the little girls asked. Jacob turned to her then dropped it onto the ground. He crushed it with his shoe and then said, "No. It's not going to be okay." The kids ran away, crying and yelling.

Jacob continued down the sidewalk until he came to the huge Iron Gate, lifted the latch, and started to enter. The sound of Doberman guard dogs barking made him run back out. He slammed the gate shut and stood waiting for someone to claim their "death on four-legs."

"Don't worry they won't hurt you." A voice called out from one of the second story balconies. He wasn't afraid of being hurt, he was afraid he'd hurt them.

"If this voice belongs to a woman with captive green-eyes, then I will step into this yard with good faith."

"On second thought, stay right there." He could hear her footsteps on the obviously wooden staircase in her mansion; the rapping of delicate toes carried out as far as the gate. She called to the puppies, which by this time, had gotten attached to the idea of biting at him. They reluctantly went inside and probably made themselves comfortable. Resting for the next time Jacob visited.

"You were saying something of my green-eyes?" Her lovely face stealing his train of thought.

"I would try to describe them, but it would be an insult to their divinity."

"Such words can get a man in trouble," she said through a coy voice.

"Now that we've properly flirted...why don't you come in?" She asked as she reached through the bars and pulled him close.

"Soon, I promise." He kissed her. Right there in front of that grand mansion, through the bars of her intimidating gate. She tasted of some delicious fruit that he had never known. It must grow wild on some far away island, he thought to himself. The rich earth and the powder blue clouds that dwell in that part of the world must feed it. Not even the natives of that region are allowed to eat of it, its flavor sampled by only kings and occasional peasants like Jacob. Men of little means and even less matters. He left that kiss, still remembered by his lips, on the other side of the gate, and he was back in the street. He stepped slowly, keeping her in mind, loving her in between breaths. The city called to him, by speaking in tongues he knew well; in the tone of an automobile horn and the whirling of machines. Jacob slipped back into the landscape, becoming another pair of eyes, temporarily too busy for love.

Chapter 27

The Balancing Game

Mia and Jacob spent the next three days together, doing only as they wished, running further and further away from their family obligations. His father's blocking of the land sale was still present in his mind, but he tried to not allow it to infect the times Mia and he had. Jacob was nervous about going home. He had asked Mia to drive him to the airport and she agreed. She had a car, he didn't. He felt uncomfortable asking her for a ride. He was still concerned with "what ifs."

She was more than happy to take him, and didn't think anything of it. She knew he didn't have money or transportation. It just didn't matter to her. Although judging from her background, money played a major role in her upbringing.

She was raised in a very wealthy family, living in mansions and attending royal galas. She was eighteen years old before she was allowed to date, her stepfather being a strict disciplinarian who kept his family jumping from one foot to the other; playing their role in that typical double standard.

Mia's mother was a kind, caring person. On their second date, Jacob was introduced to her. She welcomed him into her home with affection and genuine interest. He was escorted into the kitchen and was asked a number of questions, though she kept the conversation light and non-prying. Jacob told her of his mother's recent illness and his estrangement from his father. She extended her sympathies as well as a hug. Mia came in and told her mother some excuse, letting Jacob and her escape to the rest of their date.

The third date was a dinner at her house. Jacob was going to meet her stepfather, a well-liked businessman who had connections all over town. Everyone liked Lynch Sullivan, though they always made the distinction of "he's a great guy but a bastard when it comes to business."

After Jacob had said hello to Mia's mother, Annette Sullivan, they crept up the huge wooden stairs, slowly making their way to the abode of his 18 year old Aphrodite. She held his hand in hers and led him into the soft perfume scented room. There was a bed decorated with a large comforter, a canopy hung above, and a number of throw pillows were tossed up next to the covered sleeping pillows.

"This is a wonderful room," he said to her, looking around and finding the décor inviting.

"Thanks. You know what the best part of this room is?" She asked him as a devilish grin slid across her face.

"No, what?"

"The locks on the doors." With that she leapt over to the door and locked it. Then a second later, she was pressed against him, kissing his cold lips.

"Are you sure about this?" Taking her hands again in his and stopping the kisses.

"Of course I am. Don't you want to?"

"More than you could ever know."

"So lets."

"I have something to tell you. There's something you need to know before we do anymore."

"Shoot," she said with an impatient tone.

"I'm a v.... A vir..."

"A virgin." She quipped back.

"Well, if you have to give it a name, yes."

"I am too." He tilted his head and smiled, the pressure to perform was gone knowing that this would be memorable for the both of them. She kissed him, touching his back and sides with those soft fingers. He could feel how warm she felt to him and then he wished he could give her such warmth.

"Do you feel that?" Still kissing and fully clothed.

"What?"

"Your hands, they're warm. I've never held your hand and felt it so warm before." He put his left fingers to his right hand and found she was right.

"I feel like a normal person, I'm not an icicle." She giggled, happy to make him so excited.

"Being an icicle isn't so bad." Her eyes looking below his belt. He blushed from her gaze, moving with her towards the bed. Jacob kissed her, maneuvering around her hazelnut strands of flowing hair.

"Mia, are you in there?" It was her stepfather!

"Yeah daddy, I'm right here!"

"What's the door doing locked? Your mother says you have a gentleman in there with you."

"Yes daddy, his name is...."

"Well, have you and whatever his name is, downstairs in five minutes for dinner."

"Okay daddy." She turned to Jacob, his face strained from the panic he now felt.

"Where were we?" She asked as she continued the little tease show they were putting on for one another.

"I can't. Not with him prowling the halls." She understood that he was turned off by such an interruption, though she playfully questioned his bravery. Jacob told her it wasn't bravery that made a man make love to a woman, all the while the woman's stepfather is in the next room. It was stupidity, and thankfully, he had it in short supply. He straightened up his shirt and pants, she put a bow in her hair, and they were ready for dinner.

"I don't know how long I can stay tonight. I still haven't packed my things."

"Can I come over and help you pack?" Jacob didn't want her over there that night so he just shrugged and nodded against it.

"No problem." Her feelings were hurt and Jacob knew it. He didn't want her to go with him because he had bought her a going-away present and didn't want to ruin the surprise. He had stopped in at Ariel Sutter's Shop in Frankfort. There were racks and racks of beautifully crafted woman's clothing, all with a distinct touch from their designer, Ms. Sutter. Jacob was impressed with the young woman; honestly a bit smitten with her blue eyes and cute freckles that were sprinkled all over her milky white skin. 'You're not here to look for you goofus, you have a girlfriend. Remember?' He had reminded his wandering lust. Jacob blushed as he paid for the silky feeling dress, imagining Mia beneath its tailored cloth. Ariel knew why his ears were so red. She didn't realize that hers were too.

Mia tapped his shoulder, he had daydreamed away from her, "Shall we go then?" He pointed his bony elbow towards her. She wrapped her arm with his and they walked out of her room and down the stairs.

Jacob came into the dining room first, having led Mia down the staircase. His leather shoes clip-clopped their way across the marble floor at the bottom of the steps. He took his seat, after pulling out Mia's chair for her, thus robbing her stepfather of the opportunity. He had no malice towards Mr. Sullivan, but that's not how he took it. He glared at Jacob from the opposite end of that long elegant table. He would insist on watching Jacob relentlessly, counting each time he held Mia's hand, the number of shrimps that he put on his plate. Jacob held back much of himself that day, wanting to allow Mr. Sullivan to make an ass out of himself. Had he spoken up and possibly gotten disrespectful, Mia would have certainly shown him to the door with the intention of never seeing him again. He didn't want that. Therefore, he just sat there, smiling, waiting for him to say something out of line so that he could weave a story of his past. It would be so heart-breaking that Mia's mom wouldn't want to know her husband for the good part of a year.

Mia was quiet, unfortunately making Jacob run this gauntlet of looks and questions alone.

"So what are your plans for the future?" Lynch asked him, then took a bit of the ham onto his plate.

"I don't have a solid plan as of right now, but I have the utmost need to find such a plan."

"What does your father do?" He asked, chewing that very same ham.

"He's a farmer."

"I don't follow."

"Neither do I, but he seems to love it."

"You've never wanted to follow in that tradition?"

"No."

"So you'd never want to go home to your family's pig farm, leave Arcadia behind?"

"Actually it's not a pig farm, we mainly grow corn for feed."

"What's the difference?" Lynch asked with a sarcastic tone.

"I suppose there's no difference." Jacob looked over to Mia, telling her silently that he was ending this conversation before it got heated.

"What's that supposed to mean?" Lynch had his fork pointing at Jacob from across the table. Jacob remembered the look that the menacing darkness from his dream had given him. His cheek muscles jiggled from the tension that he felt. He wanted to jump onto the table and shove the rest of the ham down Lynch's throat. Mia's stepfather looked to her, as if she would have the answers Jacob was unwilling to voice.

"I suppose Mia has bought all of your meals and driven you around town?" Lynch was now implying that Jacob was nothing more than a gold digger.

"I've paid for our dates and have yet to be driven by her." Jacob touched her hand in plain view on the table. Lynch knew he wasn't making any progress at provoking his little girl's new boyfriend.

He shut up, looking down to his plate wishing he had asked better questions. It was too apparent now, so he didn't continue his onslaught.

Jacob looked him right in the eyes, keeping everything he did, well within his sights. He unnerved Lynch something awful, finally causing him to leave the table abruptly, drawing the puzzled looks of his daughter and wife.

Chapter 28

Drop the Disguise

"Should I go see if he's all right?" Jacob asked with fake concern.

"No dear, that's all right. He's just been under a lot of stress at work. I'm sure he'll be back to the table in just a minute." She didn't convince him any more than she convinced herself.

They finished the rest of the meal in peace and quiet, hearing only the occasional clinking of silverware. Jacob had a good time after Lynch left; though he regretted having to intimidate him so badly.

"Are you sure your stepdad's all right? I really think I should go see if he's okay." Jacob stood up and placed the napkin that had been resting on his lap, back onto the table. He stepped into the other room, crossed the marble floor, and headed back upstairs.

He finally found Lynch's office, which had a sprawling den, and library with a seriously powerful computer workstation seated in the middle.

"What are you doing here?" Lynch asked coming out from behind a shelf of books.

"I came to see if you are all right."

"How noble. Why don't you stop dicking with me and just tell me what you want? You're a day early. What's going on?"

"I don't understand what you mean…."

"Oh drop the disguise and let's just get down to business." He pressed a hidden button under his desk causing the office doors to shut then lock.

"Did you go down to the dock yet? Did you see Earl about the money?"

"I…" Jacob stopped himself from answering truthfully, seeing the loaded pistol on the desk and the heavy security around the house. If he answered wrong, this supposed "upstanding citizen" would kill him then claim he was attacking him or something.

"No," Jacob answered, "I didn't have time."

"What have you been doing? You still haven't said why you're early." He asked with a flushed red face.

"I was doing some prep work. You want this thing done right, don't you?"

"Of course. You know that's what I want. I just don't like surprises." He started to calm down, now leaning back into his chair and looking out of the huge picture window.

"Look Mr. Crane, I know this is the first time we've met, but I just can't help but feel that you're not taking this seriously."

"How's that?" Jacob replied, his heart beating out of his chest at the prospect of being called, "Mr. Crane."

"I want that bartender, Frank, dead. Not tomorrow or next year, but now!"

"Refresh my memory, why would you want a lowly bartender dead?" Jacob was now standing behind Lynch's chair with his hands in front of him.

"He's the last one on the contract." He turned around and looked Jacob in the face.

"You did get Tommy Gabberini and the thug with the gun? Right?" Jacob shook his head 'yes.' "If you do this contract right, you do it clean, then I'll give you an open agreement. You'll be able to stay in Arcadia and work again. Doesn't that sound nice?"

Jacob realized who this man was. Not only was he the stepfather of his true love, but he was the enemy of every good person in town. Jacob remembered Tommy Gabberini from one of Franks' stories. This man must be the Lumber Company executive that pissed his pants when Tommy Gabberini's thug put the gun in his mouth. Frank said a contract had been put out for Tommy G, his right-hand man, and one more person. Jacob had dismissed the notion of a final mystery target because it seemed like an obvious cliffhanger that Frank would tell just to keep him in suspense.

"When do you want it done?" Jacob asked with a new growling voice.

"I just said when. Weren't you paying any goddamned attention! I'm Lynch Sullivan! Do you know how important I am? I could buy and sell you a thousand times pal!" Jacob walked over to that oily weasel and grabbed him by the throat. He peered straight into his eyes and squeezed ever so slightly. He could hear the dripping of urine, so he didn't have to look down. Jacob gave him a displeased glance. Mr. Sullivan shut his eyes in self-loathing, so Jacob let him go.

"Don't ever talk to me like that again. You understand me?"

"Yeah." He answered.

"Yes Sir is how you answer me!" Jacob screamed at him.

"YES Sir! I'm sorry Sir!" Mr. Sullivan yelled loudly, making his voice hoarse. Jacob brushed his bangs back, the black strands getting in his way.

"I'll meet you at the rendezvous spot when it's done," said the shaken man.

"That's not going to work. You meet me at the Big Apple Bar five minutes before I do it. I'll call you when I'm about to make my move, so you better come running."

"But that's not the plan." Jacob stared back at him, telling him with his cold eyes that he was changing the plan.

"Okay, I understand, no problem."

Jacob nodded in agreement; there was no problem with this turkey, no problem at all.

Chapter 29

An Axe to Grind

The matter of the real Mr. Crane running around Arcadia with an axe to grind for his friend and countless Arcadians, didn't sit so well with Jacob.

"What were you doing with my daughter? That wasn't part of the arrangement?"

"I figured it was the only way to not look suspicious in getting to see you in person. By the way, now that you've seen my face, the price has quadrupled." He lied about his being there, not wanting to put Mia in any more danger. It seemed his love for her just might be the end of them both. Lynch's mouth hung open, his fists clenched. He wanted to argue, bitch, and moan. However, he knew only Mr. Crane's reputation and not the past of that seemingly harmless young man.

Still dazed and dripping with piss, Lynch opened the door to his office. Jacob strolled out the large entrance way and down the steps.

He went into the dining room only to find empty plates. He took a few minutes to look around, finally finding Mia and her mother outside on one of the houses' many balconies.

"Here, hold this," Mia said to him, handing him a water pitcher that she had been using to water the hanging plants.

"Could you pour some into this one?" Mrs. Sullivan asked him, pointing down to a large pottery basin and the seemingly dead plant it contained.

He soaked the soil well, even going as far as wiping off the side of the pots if he spilled any. Mia had a pair of scissors in her hands, as she clipped and trimmed leaves from a couple of different plants.

"Mia has always had a green thumb." Her mother, Annette, said bragging about her.

"She has a knack for making things better." Jacob said to Annette then looked in Mia's direction.

"I'll leave you two to finish up, I'm feeling a headache coming on."

"It was a pleasure meeting you ma'am, and thank you for the dinner. I've never had such a good home-cooked meal before." She couldn't stop smiling, even though she had her hand to her forehead in some hopes of easing the headache.

Lynch came down the steps; he had changed his soiled clothes. Jacob could hear his slippers dragging across the marble, then the carpet of the dining room. He came out onto the balcony, expecting his wife and stepdaughter, but instead found Mia and Jacob embraced in a kiss.

"Can I get anything for you two?" He asked looking at Jacob with total hatred.

"I don't believe so, but thanks for asking." Jacob said then smiled at him, then looking down at Mia. She had a worried expression on her face, as if she questioned her boyfriend's sincerity. Jacob broke the tension by saying; "I really should be going."

"Yes. What a good idea."

"Daddy!" Mia objected to his excitement for Jacob's departure.

"It's all right, I'm sure he was only kidding," his arms wrapped around Mia but his eyes stared sharply at Mr. Sullivan.

"Of course, just kidding. Ha." Neither Mia nor Jacob bought that laugh, but they just let it go.

"I'll call you later," Mia yelled to Jacob as he went back into the house, across the marble floor, and finally out the large front door. She waved to him from the balcony, giving him a taste of Shakespearean romance. Lynch glanced at Mia then scoffed off to his office. She stayed on the balcony for a while, crossing her arms and thinking about Jacob.

When the iron gates of her estate were closed behind him, Jacob hurried to the Big Apple. He had to warn Frank of Mr. Crane, assuming he didn't already know.

By the time he reached the Big Apple, Frank had closed up for the night. Jacob had never been to Frank's house before so he didn't know where to find him. He tried every coffee shop and restaurant in town but he was nowhere to be found. After spending hours and hours searching for Frank, he returned to his apartment and began to pack for his trip home.

He was able to forget the danger Frank was in just long enough to pack a change of clothes. He would be back in a day and Frank was a man who could take care of himself. He assumed that Frank knew about the hit contract and was hiding out. That made him feel not so responsible. He had tried to find him, now he needed to figure out how he would get to continue dating Mia with her stepfather believing that he is a Hitman. What happens to him when the real Mr. Crane arrives? The reasons for staying in Arcadia were fading fast; the plane ride to Bishop Springs was making more sense. Besides, he needed to see his family. The last three days with Mia had softened him up; he saw new opportunities for resolution. He had also noticed his temper was now one hundred times quicker to react.

Going to sleep that night was far more difficult than he predicted. He slept terribly as his legs ached in an uncomfortable annoyance. He couldn't feel at ease, the cold spots under the pillows disappeared as soon as he would find them.

Occasionally he would drift off but then he'd wake himself up with a sudden jerk of fear and reaction. He kept having a vision of the cute cherub from his previous nightmare. It was holding his left hand down while his right hand held a machine gun. The barrel was pointed at paper targets made in the likeness of Frank and Mia. A phantom finger pulled the trigger and the targets dropped to the ground bleeding. It was at that part that he woke up.

He finally gave up on sleeping, convincing himself to be awake for the new day when the sunrise forced orange light through the curtains. He jumped up, slid his jeans and shirt on, and clumsily put on his shoes.

He used the payphone in his apartment to call Mia, who was not already awake and sounded very groggy. She told him that she'd be there in a few minutes and then hung up the phone.

Jacob checked his carry-on knapsack and his round-trip ticket. Everything was there and so he carried himself down to the curb and waited for Mia.

While Jacob sat ready to go home, Frank was sleeping in his car's backseat. He had gone on a drinking binge and gave no reason for this to anyone that he had partied with the night before.

He woke up when the front end of his car was lifted by the tow truck that had been called to remove it. He jumped and shouted in the face of the tow truck operator but it was towed away nonetheless. His hair was standing straight up with his sweaty unshaven face looking greasy. He tucked his shirt into his pants and buttoned up his open fly. He began walking down M-22, towards the Big Apple and a fresh bottle. The sunshine made his drunken eyes ache and his teeth had a bland coating of plaque from not brushing in a while. He stuck out his thumb to get a ride, but the only car that came by didn't stop. It was a little green car with a girl driving.

Just as she had said she would, Mia was there to pick up Jacob in a few minutes, looking very sleepy and messy in her Volkswagen Jetta. It was painted green with tan interior, a large front storage compartment, and no legroom. This didn't bother Mia who stood somewhere around 5'4".

She popped the latch and Jacob tossed the bag in. He got in on the passenger seat, first lifting off her purse and a variety of girlie things that she had dumped onto the seat.

"Mia, I have something for you." He turned to the backseat and retrieved a white box with a red ribbon tied around it. She hadn't started the car, so she gave a small smile and accepted the box. He was impatient to see her open it, watching her undo the ribbon slowly. She slid her hand down the edge of the box and cut the clear tape that was keeping the top shut. She raised the top flap and lifted the dress so that she could see if better. She wept, as the black dress caressed her fingers. She couldn't wait to put it on, now doubly anxious to have Jacob come home from Bishop Springs.

"Thank you so much," she hugged and kissed him. Damn, I should have bought her a dress three days ago, he thought as she folded it back into the box. She delicately placed it in the backseat and then started the car. She felt so much better, now not solely thinking about how much she'd miss him.

She didn't want to ruin the moment but she had to remind him, "Call the airline and make sure they haven't canceled the flight." Mia pointed to the glove compartment where her cell-phone was. Jacob called the 800 number on his ticket and the Customer Service Rep told him everything was on time.

He put the phone back in the dash and rested in the reclined seat. They didn't say much on the ride there, even though they'd trade yawns and smiles.

Mia thought about how she would miss Jacob. She knew he would only be gone for a day but still she was going to miss him. She had never missed anyone really, even her last boyfriend Zack Almonds. He worked at a local campground and had the maturity of a retarded red-butted baboon. Thinking about that made her laugh out loud. Jacob looked over and just closed his eyes again. Zack had all the things that she was sure she wanted. He was good looking, funny, zany, flirtatious, and seemingly kind. Yet, he didn't romance her. He didn't appreciate the love that she gave him. He would pressure her about sex, how if she really loved him, doing it would prove it. She went out with him for the last two years of high school and when graduation day came, she broke it off. He started calling her a whore and a slut in front of her family and friends. Lynch Sullivan made a hand gesture and his bodyguards took him out of the crowd's sight. The next day, Lynch bought her that Volkswagen with a note on the dashboard that read, "To the Best Daughter in the World." Zack apologized that day, doing a good job even though his jaw had been broken and had to be wired shut. She didn't know why she was thinking of all this. Perhaps it was her way of keeping distracted before Jacob would have to leave.

"What are you thinking?" Jacob asked with one eye open.

"Nothing," she lied, "I'm just gonna miss you is all. But it's just for one day and then you'll be mine again." Jacob liked it when she said that.

Mia continued to remember odd things, like the time Zack was going to sing in front of the Lion's Club dinner. His band, Fetus Stew, was a self-described country/punk band. He wore a pair of pink sweatpants and a cowboy hat. He sang as if he was the unnatural son of Hank Williams Sr. & David Bowie. The crowd almost tar and feathered the band, but Zack's father went on stage and dragged his son off. The crowd stood up and applauded. Fetus Stew had received their first and last standing ovation.

Chapter 30

Returning Home

They made good time getting to the airport complex; it was only 10 minutes away. They drove past the departure drop-off area and continued to follow the curve until the parking structure lane began. She wanted to park in front of the terminal but it was packed as usual. Mia steered her lovebug to the automated gate and reached out of her window, snatching the ticket that marked down what time she had arrived in the lot. The wooden 2x4 arm that blocked the drive lifted up and she sped into the claustrophobic structure. She was convinced that the top of the car would hit the ceiling of the structure but somehow there was more than enough room.

Jacob had found a much closer parking spot but Mia insisted that she didn't have any room, so she kept driving up through the levels. She found one on the top level, but it was in between a badly parked mini-van and a rusty compact model. She squeezed the VW into the crooked spot and then they had to get out through the windows. Jacob was grinning from being right, but Mia didn't find it so amusing.

"You can go to the gate by yourself then." She smacked her hand on the top of the car.

"Geesh, relax. I'm just kidding around."

"Just shut up and grab your bag. We still have to get you checked in." Mia wasn't just angry about the parking job, or from thinking about Zack the moron. Most of it was her fear that Jacob would go home and not be able to come back. He didn't have any roots in Arcadia yet, and this scared the hell out of her. She was praying, without having to say it out loud, that he'd come home in a day just as he planned.

Jacob was walking with his knapsack on his shoulder and he began to mentally go over his trip list. Clothes, check. Money, check. Ticket, um, ticket, um…. Check. He found it in a zipped up pouch and stopped feeling the panic of telling Mia that he had lost the damned thing.

"Ready?" She asked.

"Ready." He answered. Mia was now determined to get him on that plane, just to prove to herself that she didn't need him. She knew he was going to see his mother, but she felt jealous and angry. In a few secret places in her mind, Mia blamed his mother for her heart problems. As if she had a hand in its' timing. Then that seemed so childish and Mia stopped indulging that way of thinking.

Now she was walking ahead of him, with her arm pulling his right elbow.

"Don't worry, it'll be fine. She'll be so happy to see you."

"I know. I can already imagine her smiling at me. What about my dad? How am I supposed to act around him? How am I going to get away again? I know he'll try to stop me from leaving. I'm sure that's why he stood in the way of the land sale."

"Just ignore him. You don't have to do anything that you don't want to do. Remember that. You're a man. Not a boy."

"You're right," he exhaled loudly, pushing back his bangs, "I love it that you are always right."

"Me too." She said.

They went through the metal detectors, taking out all their change and keys and putting them in the little plastic security trays. The guards waved them through the detectors and then they recollected their change and keys. Jacob's knapsack took a ride down the conveyor belt and through the x-ray machine. He lifted it up by its shoulder strap and walked with Mia to the gate. After checking in at the Service Desk, they took their seats in the terminal. They could see out over the tarmac and they watched the ground crews prepare the planes.

There was a strong smell of coffee and cinnamon rolls coming from a darkly lit cafe. He told her that he would be back in a second, standing up, and walking over to get them some breakfast. When he came back, she accepted the cappuccino but turned down the cinnamon roll. She said she was getting too fat. This made him give a 'are you kidding' look. She looked at the roll and wanted to taste the icing.

"I'll just try the icing." She swiped her index finger across the top and scooped up the white sugar, her finger causing cracks in the cooled confection.

"These are good." She said.

"Yes they are."

Their breakfast took only ten minutes, leaving them to wait twenty more for the plane. A young boy was sitting with this mother across the aisle from them. He had an action figure in his hand and was wearing an Italian Skiing shirt with the words, 'Quartuccio' stretched across the front. Jacob had never heard of that company but Mia recognized the name and said that they were very good skis. Jacob couldn't care less.

"I'm going to try to be less serious when I'm with you." He whispered into her ear.

"Why?" She asked.

"Because I'm poisoning this love of ours with my bullshit and my past. You don't deserve that. You deserve much, much better."

"How do you know that I'm not as much at fault for bringing us down as you?"

"Because you haven't told me any of your sob stories. I feel like that's all I ever talk to you about."

"I've never thought that. I don't think I ever will."

"I just wanted you to know that. With going on the plane, I started thinking that I might not survive. You might go on thinking something that isn't true or whole. I...love you Mia." Mia started to cry, choosing to hug him instead of wiping away her mascara that was running down her cheek. Once the moment had passed, Mia smiled and excused herself to go and re-do her makeup.

While she was gone, a father sitting behind Jacob started talking to him. He told Jacob that he was a good man for telling her that.

"Not so many people will say that and mean it. Good for you two."

"Thanks." He replied.

"Now my daughter and her idiot boyfriend are another story. He's the one with the earrings and tattoos, he just took her to go get a pop." Jacob recognized the boyfriend from earlier and wondered what the hell was going on in his head.

"I think he's trying to string my daughter out on drugs."

"What?"

"Yeah. Every time I try to talk to her, it goes nowhere. She shuts the door, hangs up the phone, or just refuses to answer me. Can you believe that?"

"You could," the man interrupts Jacob and tells him, "but I love her, you know? I want to help her but that damn guy keeps telling her lies. I wish I had a gun, I mean that with all my heart and soul."

"Wow, why don't you call the cops?"

"He'll tell them my little girl was doing it too. He even told me that's what he'd do."

"I really don't know what to tell you...I really don't."

"No hey, what am I doing? I'm sorry to dump this on you; I just needed to vent. I'm sorry."

"It's nothing to be sorry for." Mia came back with her new face and Jacob left to go to the restroom. Mia stayed behind to watch her purse and his knapsack, just like Jacob had done.

He walked into the green tiled room and noticed that the only stall was occupied. He really needed the stall after that cinnamon roll and the very strong cup of coffee. He waited patiently for his turn.

After standing there for nearly ten minutes, he lost his polite patience and spoke up, "I need to use the stall please."

"Screw off," said a man's voice.

"Whatever pal. You've had more than enough time, now get the hell out of there."

"Maybe you didn't hear me. Screw Off!" Jacob could barely hear the high pitched voice of a woman pleading with her companion for them to just leave. Then Jacob heard the slap. He lost his control over his temper and snapped. He kicked the meagerly locked stall door and reached in to grab the man. The door was jammed and he roughly pulled on the man's leather jacket.

The boyfriend hit the sinks with a thud.

"Shut the door!" He yelled to the girl. The boyfriend had his right sleeve rolled up and a piece of rubber tubing tied around his right bicep.

"Heroine? You piece of shit!" Jacob slammed his head into the restroom wall, breaking squares of green tile. The girl just sat there listening from behind the stall door, as Jacob beat and broke her boyfriend. Once there were a group of cuts and bruises on the boyfriend's face, Jacob turned to the girl.

"Did you shoot up?"

"What?" The girl asked, too scared to think.

"The Heroine. Did you do any?"

"No. He said sharing my first hit would be romantic."

"Romantic?" Jacob couldn't believe his ears.

"He's not just about drugs. He's going to be a writer." Jacob rolled his eyes.

"Let me tell you something. Writers are the most dangerous people in the world. Stay away from them."

"What was I supposed to do? Say no?"

"You're goddamned right!" Jacob yelled at her, then calmed. He picked up her things and sent her out to her father. He told her not to say anything, he knew she wouldn't.

He locked the restroom door behind him and slid the unconscious boyfriend into the stall. There were four packets of Heroin in the boyfriend's jacket, along with a bent-burnt spoon that he'd gotten at the cafe. The boyfriend was waking up so Jacob took his opportunity to make a point.

"Can you hear me? You sick bastard. If you ever go near that girl again, I will kill you. You understand me? You ever go near another girl with drugs again, I will doubly kill you."

"Ahhhh." The boyfriend groaned and Jacob took that as an agreement.

While Jacob was dealing with the boyfriend, the girl kept her mouth shut and walked away from the locked restroom. Her makeup was smeared from the frightening past minutes, adding a great theatrical touch to the story that she was going to tell her dad. She sat down next to him and told him about her "break up." He comforted her, while Mia went into her purse for some Kleenex. Jacob came back to the sitting area, watching the girl cry, feeling good about what he had just done.

"There you are. Where've you been?" Mia asked. The crying girl looked up and then straight back down. She was ashamed of herself and she was afraid of Jacob.

"Is that blood on your sleeve?" Mia asked, turning his sleeve to the left then the right as she examined it.

"No, it's ketchup. Some kid bumped me with his lunch."

"It is crowded in her. Just a little longer and you'll be flying through the wild blue yonder." Jacob just smiled. He couldn't share in her enthusiasm for going home. Instead, he thought about Frank and the restroom scene.

"That was cool." He accidentally said aloud.

"What was cool?" Mia asked. The crying girl and her father looked over at him. Both were wondering what he meant.

"Oh it's nothing. Forget it."

Around the time the plane landed and began to unload its arriving passengers, Jacob saw a group of security guards enter the men's restroom. A minute or two passed, and then five more guards arrived. They had the boyfriend handcuffed behind his back and they were radioing into the station that they had a possible overdose. One of the guards told the person on the other end of the radio that the man being arrested had all the telltale signs of Narcotic Psychosis. He had torn up the bathroom and himself, or so the theory went.

"Isn't that...?" The father pointed at the ex-boyfriend.

"Don't look dad, just let them take him away."

"What the hell's going on Stacey?"

"I'll tell you later dad. I promise. Let's just go back home." She put her head down and he sat there confused.

"Okay honey, you know your room is always there for you." He carried her purse and bag, letting her lean against him as they went back to their car.

"Flight 101, to St. Paul Minnesota will be boarding in five minutes. Ground Team please set the stairs." The PA system cracked and then there were no further announcements.

"It's almost time. These people have to get off and get their baggage, then you can get on." Mia was acting weird. She was faking excitement on his leaving. His mother had been sick before and she turned out fine. He tried to warn Frank about Lynch Sullivan but he was sure Frank knew about it. Frank had most likely told Jacob just enough to be interesting, not enough to be true.

He couldn't tolerate sitting anymore, so he slung his bag over his shoulder and walked to the large windows overlooking the tarmac. Mia followed and took a position to his right. A group of men arrived at the gate without bags, but had name placards instead. They were limo drivers and Jacob quickly read over the names. None of them were famous.

People started walking up the long inclined corridor. There were military personnel with their new boot camp haircuts and razor sharp manners. Scattered around them were the senior citizen vacationers with their new straw hats that they'd never wear again. Jacob and Mia held hands and stood back from the corridor's entrance since the people arriving and the people picking them up, were dropping their things in the doorway just to say hi and hug.

Jacob looked back into the airport terminal while the people continued to be off loaded. A semi-chubby man ran up to the group of limo drivers and held up his sign. He was out of breath and had a sweaty forehead. His placard was shaking and moving, so Jacob looked even harder. It was steadied for just a few seconds, long enough to read "Crane."

His heart was in his throat, but he slowly drew in a lungs' worth and then exhaled it. Mia heard him and she thought he was just trying to relax. Final groups of passengers were walking slowly up the corridor. They were all businessmen, wearing their pink polo shirts and white shorts. Jacob stood on his tiptoes but there wasn't anyone else walking up the ramp.

"You are nervous," said Mia. Jacob ignored her and kept looking. At that moment, Jacob saw a tall thin man in a black overcoat, which went up to the man's neck, walking out of the plane and into the corridor. He stared closer, seeing the man make his way up to where the rest of the people were. The man in black walked by Jacob and Mia, heading over to take a seat. It appeared that he was waiting for a ride.

"Okay time to go." Mia started to guide him to the corridor.

"Not yet. Just wait." He was watching the man in black, as he unbuttoned his coat and opened it. He could now see that the man in black was wearing a priest's collar.

"Oh shit." Jacob slipped in saying.

"Jacob!" Mia chirped.

"Sorry, I...uh forget it. I have to go." He leaned down, kissed her soft lips, and stared into her lovely green eyes.

"Be safe. I'll see you soon." They hugged, leaving Mia's head resting on his shoulder. He was now looking at the limo driver holding the "Crane" sign. The driver turned to the priest then nodded once, then the priest nodded twice.

At this point, Mia had let go of Jacob and tearfully walked alone out of the terminal. Jacob kept waiting to the last possible second before he would have to get on the plane. He was watching the priest tidy up his things, folding his newspaper in half. Then suddenly someone tapped him on the shoulder.

"Hey kid!" It was Frank!

"What are you doing here Frank?"

"I'm seeing you off. You surprised?" He smelled of booze and sweat. He had washed his face and combed his hair but he still looked like crap.

"Yeah I'm surprised."

"Good cause that's what I was shooting for."

"Frank listen to me," Jacob led him over to the large windows and leaned in to whisper, "Do you recognize anyone else in this terminal?" Frank turned around and examined the faces of the people. His eyes worked left to right until abruptly, he spun back around.

"That's Crane!" He said with a panicked tone.

"Christ!"

"It's him. I know it's him." Frank turned around again studying the priest. He had the same shape and demeanor as the young Crane that he had known. He was just older and had a few streaks of gray in his hair. Frank felt sick.

"Lynch Sullivan hired him," Jacob told Frank, "he's going to kill you for the same reason he killed Gabberini." Frank shook his head, as if he was expecting this.

"Get on the plane kid. There's nothing you can do. Just go. Don't come back here." Frank pushed him to the corridor and then speedily walked past the man he believed was Mr. Crane. Jacob couldn't yell to him, he couldn't take the chance of getting Mr. Crane's attention. Jacob stood there with a ticket to go home, to get away from all the danger.

"Sir, you really need to board now," said the gate attendant.

"I'm not going," Jacob said to her as he tucked the ticket into his jacket pocket.

Jacob did all that he could to not be seen by Frank. He knew that if he were seen, Frank would make him get on the plane or at least stay out of town. Jacob believed he could help, he would just talk Frank into going out of town, and then he would call the Feds. They'd arrest Mr. Crane and would find a weapon on him. That would give the Feds an excuse to hold him until Frank could be better hidden.

He thought about what he'd say to Frank when he'd walk into the bar and would show that he wasn't on a plane for home. Jacob walked out of the airport and flagged down a taxi.

"How much to Arcadia?"

"Ten bucks."

"Let's go then." He got into the back and slid the ten through the money slot. The cabby flipped the meter on and they left for home.

"Where exactly in Arcadia?" The cabby asked him.

"The Big Apple Bar."

"Oh yeah, I know that place."

"Yeah me too."

The taxi dropped him off in the parking lot and the gravel spit into the air when the taxi driver gassed the engine. Jacob gave him an impatient look then tried the door to the bar. It was locked. He peered around the parking lot and saw five very expensive cars. There was a clicking sound coming from the back of the bar and so Jacob went to see if Frank was making the noise. Jacob knocked on the back door, telling the guy at the door that he had to talk to Frank. Though the room was filled with cigar smoke, he could see Frank, who also had just arrived at the poker table. Frank was working on his first hand and it looked to be the start of a lucky night. The dealer looked up to Jacob, then continued the game. He followed the filthy wall until he found a stool leaning against the far corner. He took his seat and waited for the hand to be over. Frank had a pair showing, choosing to see the bet then raise. The clicking sound of the handful of bet chips filled the room, making the other players shift in their seats. All but one of them was familiar to him, being regulars that he had seen every day during the time he'd spent in Arcadia.

The one that he didn't know said he was a baker when he was a younger man. You would never think it to look at him. He had a pinstriped suit, high polished shoes, and enough gold on his wrists and fingers to finance a small revolution. Jacob kept his eyes on his jewelry and left the game to be played by those holding cards.

The baker called Franks bet and then raised a full stack of hundred dollar chips. Frank hesitated for about a half-second then pushed his entire stack of chips into the pot. The baker flipped over his cards, revealing three aces and a pair of 8's. A dead man's hand. Frank looked over at the one-time baker, as if someone had walked over his grave. He turned the cards over one-by-one, showing the room full of poker faces a stone-cold hand, a royal flush.

The baker let out a loud sigh; the other men congratulated Frank on a good hand. Frank grinned; looking down to his chips then saw Jacob sitting there, eager to speak.

"What the hell are you doing here?" Frank was drunk off his ass, finding it hard to simply sit in his chair. How he won that hand is a mystery. "I put you on that plane boy! I told you. Leave! Didn't I?"

"Yes Frank you did."

"All right then, just as long as that's noted and recorded." He pointed his drunken finger at all the men in the room as if they were witnesses to some great cosmic statement. Jacob couldn't fathom why he would just sit there playing poker, knowing that Mr. Crane would soon arrive to finish his contract.

"We need to talk."

"In a while kid, I'm on a winning-streak." He rubbed his hands together, drying them the best way available.

"No Frank, now." Frank tilted his head up to see him fully, then collected his chips and cashed out. The other men at the table complained and moaned about losing their chance to win their money back. Jacob didn't care.

"I'm screwed," Frank said into his hands, which covered his face.

"You just giving up? Are you just gonna sit here and drink yourself into a coma, so it doesn't hurt when Crane puts a bullet in your head? It's time to figure out what we're gonna do."

"A plan? You think you can outsmart a guy who's been doing contract hits his whole life." He was desperate, keeping his face buried in his sweaty palms.

"You don't have it in you to kill him do you?" Jacob asked.

Frank looked in Jacob's eyes and said, "you think you do?" Jacob didn't answer him.

"Come on, let's go out front and have a drink." Frank suggested.

"You go first, I've got to get a change of clothes upstairs." So he ran up the still wet steps, jiggled his doorknob, and walked into his room. Everything was the way he left it, all scattered throughout the room without a stitch of order. Everything went dark as the club struck his head and he fell to the floor with a thud.

Chapter 31

▼

The Moonlight Swim

Jacob awoke in Elberta harbor, on one of the many docks that wrapped the beaches. He received a smack to the face and was alive once more. It was dark out but the light from the dock lampposts shone on him and the men who kidnapped him.

"So you thought you could double-cross me?" The voice of Lynch Sullivan, Mia's stepfather, asked. He walked towards the edge as Jacob sat duct taped and shackled to a metal-framed chair. His arms and legs were immobilized by the restraints. Only his fear was free to roam.

"You took the package from Earl. I want it back."

"What package? You've got the wrong man."

"Don't play games boy. I know you're young but I won't underestimate you. We found Earl's body in the refrigerator at his place. That was two hours ago. Goddamn you work fast; I'll give you that. He didn't have the briefcase with him. You weren't supposed to kill him, he was just a carrier."

"Look, I didn't kill anyone. I'm not who you think I am. Really. This isn't a trick. It the God's honest truth. I'm just a barback. No more, no less."

"This coyness is very entertaining. You really play this part well." Jacob looked over the faces of the three other men on the pier, standing there with pistols tucked under their suits.

"I don't know what you want me to say."

"Tell me where to get my f——-ing money!" Jacob sat there quickly assessing this awful situation. The men were standing around him, barely holding back their urges to beat him to death.

"I made up my mind, I'll tell you where I hid it."

"Finally. Where?"

"It's down there." Jacob tilted his head to the dark depths below the dock.

"Really?"

"Indeed." He grinned at Lynch, deciding that if he was to die as Mr. Crane, he might as well allow his last minutes to be lived as such.

"Well, what are you waiting for? Help him get my money." Lynch said coldly to his men, telling them to pick Jacob up and toss him into the water below. Jacob began to hyperventilate as they placed a plastic bag over his head. He held his breath as he could feel them getting near to the dock's edge. Jacob released that pent-up air, trading it for a fresher amount.

"No holding your breath," one of the thugs said, right before he punched him squarely in the stomach. Jacob felt the velocity of falling, then the sudden stop of the cold water. He looked through the clear plastic hood and saw the dock's pillars encrusted with soil from the marina. The bag, which clung to his terrified head, had been tied below the chin, leaving him with a minute's worth of air. If he were unable to fix this unfortunate moment, he would forever sit at that harbor's murky bottom.

Jacob was thankful for the duct tape and not chains, for the water lifted the glue from the tape and allowed him to have free hands. However, on his ankles attached before the length of his leg's muscle, was a pair of police shackles. He breathed slowly, his heart beating like he'd never felt before. He removed the belt from around his waist and used the fastening pin to pick at the inner works of the cuffs. He focused on the bubbles that leaked out from under his chin, rising along the surface of the bag and upward to freedom.

"You think he's dead yet?" One of the thugs asked aloud, stirring the anger of his boss.

"No. I think he's taking his time. Perhaps having a meal and a show." He glared back at the dimwitted thug. They continued to look down below, the air bubbles becoming few and far between.

Jacob wrangled the pin into the firm lock that bound him to the steel chair; looking upwards, in the hopes that his desire was enough to release him. He could feel the light-headed dizziness of a drowning man, the bag now half full of water and rising. He yanked and yanked until the cuffs cut his frantic leg.

The young man continued to poke and prod with the pick, hoping to get lucky and not die such a helpless death. The bag was a moment away from completely flooding, forcing him to take the remaining air into his lungs and hold it. He held his lips together with survival fortification. The aching in his chest increased as he flirted with "just letting go." Nevertheless, he wouldn't, because Frank needed him and Mia wanted him.

He envisioned the farm, Arcadia, Mia, then the violent dreams he'd been having. The image of Mia murdered by his darker half or the cherub appeared in his mind and he felt an itch near the cuffs. He violently fought off dying at these men's request. He twisted the pin and the awaited on cuff released. He swam with blood running down his right ankle and along his foot. He left behind the steel chair and a very near miss.

The air rushed into his lungs, causing a sharp and dry pain. Waterlogged and fighting off the urge to cough and hack, Jacob pushed the water away from him, treading beneath the pier, hidden by the natural nighttime darkness. He wanted those four men dead. Not a thought of forgiveness or conscience interrupted his mind. He hated them and would prove it so by putting two bullets in each of them.

He climbed the brace supports that interconnected the pillars, finding a spot near the edge that afforded him some cover. One of the goons was standing on the pier above him, with his shiny shoes gleaming from the lamppost light. Jacob silently crept up to arm's reach and grabbed the goons' pinstriped tie. With his soaked hand, he pulled the man over the edge.

As the goon fell, his arm caught the rail and he held on. Jacob put his hand into the man's suit and retrieved the pistol that had been brandished in his face before he was tossed in. He pointed the gun to the man's heart and fired. The blood shot against the pillar, the man's body fell dead. The others, now alert and armed to deal with Jacob in a most unkind way, fired into the floorboards that held them above. Jacob climbed to another pillar, and then he crept over the edge, remaining in the shadow of the pier unlit up by the lamppost.

"Come on kid. No hard feelings, right?" Lynch called out to him. He touched the shoulders of the thugs, ordering them around the pier in the hopes of taking Jacob's life. Jacob nursed the gun and its 12 rounds with an affection he had never shown. He depended on this piece of steel to stop the death that was meant for him.

He pointed the barrel with his prone hands and fired into the remaining thugs. They dropped, having two bullets each rattling around their heads. Lynch just stood there, hands in his pocket and an unlit cigarette in his mouth.

Jacob walked to him, the water running off his soaked pants and heavy shoes. The gun was pressed against Lynch's throat, distracting him from the punch Jacob had thrown. The soaking wet killer found the duct tape roll more vengeful than the gun, so he made Lynch a permanent fixture to the car. Lynch woke to find himself attached to the automobile, hands taped to the steering wheel, his head held back to the chair.

"What are you doing? You crazy bastard." Jacob leaned down and made a sniffing sound with his nose.

"You smell that? Smells like…. Gas." He smiled, then took the car out of gear, pushing it down the dock and over the edge. It stopped as it tilted back and forth on the end of the dock, the gas tank open with a tube hanging from it. The draining gasoline had left a trail; from where Jacob was, to the edge of the dock. He put Lynch's unused cigarette into his own mouth and lit it. Jacob took a few drags and then dropped it. The flame flashed across the wooden planks then ignited the Cadillac with Mia's stepfather inside. The glass and metal compartments were filleted off the frame, spreading out over the dark water as the gasoline set the harbor on fire. Jacob turned his back to the engulfed dock and felt no regrets.

"That wasn't so bad," Jacob said to himself. He looked down at his blood-covered clothes, feeling the stickiness of it all. His hands were only shaking a bit. "These were my favorite pants. Damn it, now they're ruined."

Around the same time as Jacob's traumatic swim, Emily and Doyle James were in Bishop Springs Memorial Hospital, discussing Emily's funeral arrangements.

"You're not going to die, Emily. Jesus. You've just got a few heart problems, the doctors already said you'd be fine."

"Doyle, I love you. But shut up. I have a bad feeling. I can't explain it and I can't make it go away. I feel like death is just around the corner."

"Emily, you're scared. I'm scared too."

"I want you to go and get Jacob. Bring him home. I've got to see him before I die."

"Jesus, are you not listening?" Doyle was frustrated and was about to go and get the twenty-year old doctor that was seeing to his wife's health.

"Doyle. I mean it. Go and bring Jakey home." He sat at the foot of her bed and said, "I haven't heard you call him Jakey in a long time."

"I know." Doyle rubbed his chin a number of times then opened his eyes very wide as to wake himself from the melancholy attitude that he had taken on. The hospital stink was getting to him and secretly he was happy about the idea of going and bringing Jacob home. He thought Emily was supporting his view of where Jacob should live. Emily knew this and set something straight, "I want to see him, but he needs to go back to Arcadia when the visit is over." Doyle was not pleased.

"Fine, I'll go early tomorrow morning. I'll have Jilly pick me up and take me to the boy."

"Good. Now that's settled, I want to sleep."
"Whatever Emily."
"Goodnight Doyle."
"Night."

Chapter 32

▼

Mr. Crane Comes to Town

It was eerily quiet as Jacob finished the long walk home, pulling out the business card that Lynch Sullivan had given to him. It had 'Earl/555-9688' written on the back. There were a few bloody fingerprints on the back.

Jacob rushed up the stairs and shut the door. He quickly scrubbed off the blood and washed down in the shower. He bagged his clothes and placed it near the door. He put on a fresh set of clothes and ran down the stairs again, dragging the bag of bloody garments. He tossed the evidence into the Big Apple's incinerator and made his way back to the entrance of the bar. It was quiet inside, since the weather was so nice; no one was in the mood to stay indoors. Jacob thought that it was later in the day than it really was. The bar was closed but the lights were still on.

Frank was sitting in the bar with his feet propped up on a table, his dirty hands wrapped around a bottle of whiskey. Jacob raced into the room, nearly making Frank jump out of his seat.

"Damn kid. What the hell are you trying to do to me?" Frank said, putting his hands to his chest.

"I've got to give you something." Jacob reached into his jacket pocket and pulled out the gun from the dock.

"It's the answer to our prayers. I need you to clean it and then get me some more bullets for it."

Frank just looked at him. It didn't matter what Jacob had said, Frank wasn't hearing anything. The booze was running fast and furious through his veins. It was because of this impairment that he took the gun request so much better than Jacob had predicted. Jacob got closer, finding Frank's eyes bloodshot and teary.

"Come on Frank, you've got to sober up." He tried to lift him up, wanting to get some coffee in him. Frank's legs suddenly went limp, allowing him to fall to the ground. Jacob shook him, "Frank what's the matter? Frank!"

He just laid there, eyes looking up to some point in space.

"Come on Frank wake the hell up!" He smacked his unshaven face, jostled his old body.

"Please Frank, please…" He just lay there motionless. Jacob turned from Frank's body and stared into his hands. He pictured the mysterious Mr. Crane putting poison into the whiskey bottle.

Thinking about what he was going to do, he didn't notice Frank sitting up. "What are you blubbering about?" Frank asked him, still holding onto the whiskey bottle.

"Frank! You're not dead!"

"Do I look dead to you, Mr. Writer?"

"No, I'd say you're something, but definitely not dead."

"Good, now help me up. You look like crap, you want some?" He held the wet end of the bottle towards Jacob. Jacob shook off the offer and took the bottle from him, then set it on the floor.

"What were you saying?" His mind too pickled to remember. He blinked his tired eyes at the young man, focusing on his shirt as he thought.

"We don't have to worry about Lynch Sullivan anymore."

"Oh?" Frank asked.

"You don't want to know."

"You're right, I don't."

"Then sober up because we've got to get some sort of a plan together."

"You think I don't know that. I've just got to think, figure a way out of this."

"I think I have a way to solve all of our problems. I'll do the bloody stuff, if you do your part. It involves throwing a party."

"What?" He asked confused.

"You've just got to trust me. Spread the word that there's to be a huge party tomorrow night, a Big Apple going out of business party."

"Going out of business party?"

"Yeah, cause look. Crane loves an audience, right? He'll definitely be here just so that you don't take off and leave the country. So you see, a party is just what we need. That, and some more bullets." Again, he pushed the gun in Frank's direction, wishing he would get started.

Frank gave Jacob such a bad feeling, having to be persuaded to save his own life. They just had to make sure they didn't get someone innocent killed.

He helped Frank onto his feet; the realization of Crane's close arrival sobered Frank up quicker than any pot of coffee. He sat at the bar, a rag and cleaner in his hungover hands. Fifteen minutes later, Frank had a fully cleaned and loaded 9mm Beretta in his hands. He glanced over to the clock and began to countdown the minutes until either he or Crane would be dead.

Chapter 33

▼

The Velvet Rope Was Gone

Jacob sped upstairs to his place, checking behind the door for anymore surprise guests. He found the apartment in its usual condition and collected his hidden money; which was kept in an envelope in his closet, right under a spare blanket. He ran to the window and scanned the street, not seeing a tall-lanky man in a black suit and being totally grateful for Mr. Crane's fashion sense. It would be Crane's signature on his own hit contract.

Like all other days, the stairs outside his apartment were moss covered and wet. He didn't have time to stop and observe it in detail, so you'll have to take my word for it.

The city was filling with tourists, Heritage Days 1990 started in two days, and the streets were already getting cramped. Even with the busy sidewalks and gauckers shopping, Jacob made it to Mia's, in the vain attempt of delivering a letter. Lynch Sullivan had supposedly left town for a "business trip," which was his idea of an alibi. He had chartered a private plane and was planning to leave the country, just as soon as Jacob was dead. Instead, his plan backfired and now he was doing his part to save the environment. His body was now feeding all sorts of little fishes.

Mia's mom, Annette, answered the gate, forcing the growling Dobermans back into the house. She called Mia down, talking to Jacob as he waited. She asked if something was wrong, giving extra attention to his sweaty face. He assured her that he was fine, just not a hot weather person. She told him it was the humidity, he just nodded.

Mia ran down the steps as Jacob ran up them, meeting somewhere in the middle, kissing each other with a frustrated hunger.

"What are you doing here? I thought you got on the plane?" She was surprised to see him.

"I couldn't. I probably should've but I didn't."

"Do you want to do something tonight?" She asked him with an eyebrow raised.

"Tonight. Sure. If you want." He replied paranoid, looking back over his shoulder.

"What time are you going to pick me up?"

"I can't talk about that now. I only have a few minutes, but you've got to promise me that you'll stay home until I come and get you."

"What's wrong?" Mia said, puzzled.

"I put everything in this letter…just keep it for me, and if something happens to me, give it to the FBI."

"The FBI?"

"Yeah, they won't be easily bribed, not like the connected cops around here." She just kept staring at him, getting scared with every cryptic answer.

"Promise me, Mia, please."

"I promise, but you have to do something for me." Jacob kept looking at the front door, waiting for a black suit and a gun to be seen.

"Fine anything." He haphazardly replied.

"Tell me you love me."

"Oh, I love you so much."

"How much?"

"More than the moon and the stars." She didn't know what to say, neither did he. They kept standing on that staircase, just waiting for the other to speak.

"I love you Mia. I truly do, no matter what happens, no matter what you hear about me."

"What could I possibly hear that would make me stop loving this face?" She squashed his cheeks together and kissed his smooshed lips.

"I have to go." Jacob let go of her, he felt sick for holding her with the same hands that killed her stepfather. She yelled to him, "Your hands have gone cold. What's that about?"

"Mia, not even I know what the hell's going on." With that unfortunate farewell, he was back outside.

Never mind his travels from Mia's house to the bar, there's no time for that. What's important is he got there on time and ready to go. Jacob took a final deep breath, then jerked the door open, and took his place behind the bar. He served five tables before he glanced over to the darkened booth.

There was smoke coming from that usually empty corner. The velvet rope was gone, and all he could make out with real clarity, was a pair of shiny black dress shoes and a briefcase resting under the table.

Frank was out on the floor, busing tables and taking orders, even taking time to drink a cold pop in between tables. Jacob came over to him and patted him on the back, feeling the wet spot along his spine.

"I guess I am just a little nervous." He laughed; shaking off the creeps he felt and kept working. He and Jacob worked the floor that night better than they had ever done before, barely messing up drinks or making change.

Doyle James had arrived in Arcadia just thirty minutes prior and had been picked up by Jilly. She was uncomfortable about driving her uncle to surprise Jacob at work. She knew Jacob didn't want to go home and she anticipated a fistfight between the two. Doyle made remarks about the soil in Arcadia, commenting on the set ups the local farmers were using. Some of the ideas were very original and he couldn't wait to get home to try them out.

"Is he doing good? Jacob that is."

"Yeah I know who you're talking about. He's doing well. He likes his job and has a place of his own."

"That's what he said on the answering machine."

"Yep." Jilly bopped her head in agreement. They were traveling northbound on M-22, driving over the bridge and were within eyesight of the bar.

"There it is, but I've got to go to my house real quick. I need to give Jacob something before he leaves."

"Okay, just as long as we make the last flight out for tonight."

"Oh, you'll have plenty of time." They drove by and then turned left on Division Street. She pulled up into her driveway and parked the car.

"Can I use your restroom?" Doyle asked.

"Sure uncle." She took out her keys and opened the door. He went in and used the bathroom while Jilly got on the phone to the Big Apple. The line was busy. She tried again, and this time Frank answered.

"Hello, Big Apple Bar, Frank speaking."

"Frank, this is Jilly. You know? Jacob's cousin!" Frank covered the phone and called Jacob over to the bar counter.

"Your cousin is on the phone."

"Take a message. I can't talk to her now." Frank returned to talking to Jilly, "Can I take a message young lady?"

"Tell him his father is here in Arcadia and is going to come and take him home." Frank hung up his end of the line. Jilly just stared into the receiver and then placed it down on the catch. Uncle Doyle came out of the restroom; refreshed and ready to get Jacob.

"I'm expecting a phone-call uncle, it'll just take a few minutes."

"I can walk over there, it's not far."

"Nonsense, I'll just drive you over there after my call. It probably won't be but five minutes."

"Okay." He sat down on her couch and hummed to himself. Doyle was missing the farm already. He was worried about the guy he put in charge of things. Second guessing those workers wasn't a bad idea. Many of them were dumber than a bag of hair trying to be a bag of dirt. Doyle just wanted to get the boy and go home.

Chapter 34

In That Darkened Booth

Frank gave Jacob the message and watched as the coloring drained from his face. Jacob tilted to his left then right. Frank was sure he would pass out. Jacob took a sip of ice water and that made the nauseous hot flash leave him. He picked up his receipt book and his tray. It was showtime.

He was genuinely panic-stricken as he went over to Mr. Crane's table and asked him if he would like anything else. He heard a low-voice, so soft and quiet that he had to lean in to hear the last part of what he was saying.

"Send Frank over with an Absinthe," said the mysterious voice.

"Well sir, Frank's pretty busy, how about I get it for you?" Jacob rushed over to the bar before he could voice any objections. He slid a glass off the rack, then put it with the Absinthe bottle on his tray, as well as a clean spoon and a few sugar cubes.

"Here you are sir, oh look at that I spilled your drink all over the table. Here, I'll go get my wiping towel. I'll be right back." Jacob ran back over to the bar trying to convince Mr. Crane that he was as incompetent as they come. He just had to keep moving, in case Mr. Crane was pissed off and decided to take a shot at him too.

"Here you are sir, one wiping towel." He said to the dark corner and naively took his time in wiping up the mess.

"Are you impaired in some way?" The low-toned voice said from its shadow.

"Not that I know of, but I do have webbed feet." He said, taking on a persona of a waiting staff moron.

"Just finish wiping up and get the hell out of my face!"

"Yes sir, yes sir. I do apologize for my sloppiness, I sometimes move too quick for my own good."

"I have the same problem." Crane's words growled. Jacob slid into the booth; right next to him, finding it was only the two of them in that dark little booth.

"Really? Cause I've always wanted to talk with someone who's had to go though the same sort of…"

"Enough!" Crane slid out the other end of the booth and walked over to Frank who was waiting on some customers.

"This son of a bitch has been talking my god damned ear off." Frank looked at the darkened booth, then looked up to the face of Mr. Crane.

"What and who are you talking about sir? There's no one there."

"What the fu…" Crane turned around and stared into the dark corner, unable to see anyone.

"He was just here. Two damn seconds ago. He served me a drink and then spilled it all over the table."

"Sir, I'm the only one who works here." Frank looked at Mr. Crane, giving him the performance of a lifetime. Crane just whipped his head around, scanning the rest of the faces that decorated the bar. Nothing. He didn't see Jacob, or anyone that remotely looked like him. He went back to Frank, putting his finger on his forehead; "I'll be seeing you soon." Frank didn't say a word.

Crane turned to get his coat and briefcase from the booth, nearing it with every step, checking under the table for legs and obvious feet. He didn't see anyone.

He leaned into the shadowy corner, finding the scent of gun oil midway through the dark. "It's no gold bullet, but it'll do." The air became filled with blood and skull fragments, powder and noise. The shot scared the unaware patrons to the floor. They clenched their eyes shut, their ears filled with ringing echoes.

"Oh my god!" Frank rushed to the man's body, checking for any sign of life. The blood pool spread out evenly on the floor as Frank ran to the phone behind the bar and telephoned the cops.

They got there five minutes later; the parking lot was filled with crying women and a thousand stories that were trying to explain what happened to the mutilated body. Frank had been outside with the people, comforting them while holding back the fear.

The officers secured the crime scene and used yellow police tape to block off the entrance. Frank stepped inside to tell the cops that an ambulance would not be necessary. The man on the floor was dead.

He stayed inside and knelt next to the body, grasping the cold hand with a disappointed look on his face. The cops asked him, "Do you know this man?" He couldn't recognize the face but the clothes were very familiar.

"Yes sir, I know who that is." The detectives raised their shoulders; "It's my employee. His name was Jacob."

He had to take a seat in a booth; the last fifteen minutes had robbed him of sturdiness. He was facing the glass door and saw the police keeping people from entering the bar, which was now an official crime scene. He put his right hand up to his right cheek and leaned against it although it was shaking uncontrollably.

The sirens from the cop cars had blared down M-22, getting the attention of Jacob's father, in addition to other citizens of the sleepy little village.

"I'm going over there now."

"Here, I'll take you. That call doesn't look like it's coming anytime soon." She had lied about the call in order to give Jacob a head start, assuming he wanted to run away. She had no idea that day would end in murder.

They pulled up onto the right shoulder and Doyle jumped out. There were people and police staring at the bar, cop cruisers flashing their lights. Frank slowed his shaking arms the best he could, but the witnessing of a murder made his hangover seem permanent. He was focusing on the faces in the crowd, whether it was the cops or the people who came running when the sirens arrived. A lone man in the crowd got his attention. He recognized the man from a picture Jacob had shown him, remembering the face of Doyle James.

Doyle's overalls and flannel shirt made him sweat tremendously as he neared the entrance. He told the guard at the door that he was the father of an employee and was let through the yellow tape, which stopped at the outside of the entrance. He saw the shoes that his brother-in-law had given to Jacob. He was standing there for only a second before he burst into tears. He had recognized the dead man's clothes, as those of Jacob's. The identification in the man's pockets was those of Jacob George James. He looked the billfold over, finding a picture of his wife and himself missing. He put his hands to his head and he asked God, "How do I tell his mother?" God did not answer. Apparently, he wasn't taking questions that day. The TV crews got a shot of Doyle weeping; it was a money shot for the viewers.

The lead detective came into the bar and stood in front of Frank as he sat there shaking.

"What happened here Frank?" Frank looked up, then pointed to the booth where Crane had always hid.

"Just business as usual." The cop cleared his throat, placing his left hand on the holster of his gun while he turned to walk away.

"Tell Mr. Crane that I send my highest regards."

"I will." The detective walked out of the bar and into the parking lot, where he told the reporters that it had been a robbery-gone-bad, resulting in the death of a promising young man. It was exactly as Frank said. It was just business as usual.

With the body put on a stretcher and a trail of blood spilled out the door and into the ambulance, the police ended their investigation; sure of what had happened. The investigating detective closed the Case before they even left the parking lot. Doyle and Jilly were taken to the police station in order to officially claim and arrange for the young man's remains. That sobbing farmer sat in the back of the police cruiser and wept into his niece's shoulder.

The police began to clear the parking lot and unsealed the door to the Big Apple, leaving only Frank inside to clean up. Well, Frank and an unseen man in the darkened booth.

After the appearance of Jacob's father, the police had a positive ID on Jacob's body; dental records would not be used since the man took a 9mm hollow point bullet in the face at point blank range. Just one bullet was fired, as everyone had said all along. The cops could use that to establish a cover-up for the crime, making the citizens believe that a stranger had come into town looking for easy money and tried to rob the bar. Although the cops didn't know why Mr. Crane had killed the young man, they knew not to ask too many questions.

The sobbing women's tears in the street and parking lot were uncomfortable to listen to and it made the officers want to go home, if only to escape the crying. The killer had crept back into the darkened booth before the police arrived, lifting the briefcase up to his beating chest. The cops knew The Big Apple very well, so they thought nothing of the blacked out booth or the velvet rope that surrounded it.

Frank went over to the booth after the cops left, seeing the crimson liquid and the whitish-gray brain matter sprayed all over. He reached in to grab Mr. Crane's glass when a cold hand grabbed him. He shouted and screamed as he fell backwards onto the spot where the body had just recently been. He slipped and slid on the blood, trying to get as far away from the booth as possible.

At that moment, Mia came through the door. She had arrived just minutes after the cops had left, breaking the protective ribbon outside of the door in order to get in. The bell that hung on the door rang as she stepped in. It seems she saw the police cars and got worried. She had turned on the TV and a live report told her who had allegedly died. In her panic, she opened the letter that Jacob had left, and read his account of the corner booth hitman's tales. He had wanted her to know whom, if anyone, was responsible for his murder, if that unfortunate incident should occur. At the bottom of his hand-printed message it said, "If I'm dead, make sure you don't forget me."

So there she stood, green-eyes twinkling with fresh tears, having heard the name of the dead man now on his way to the morgue. She had been drawing conclusions all the way to the bar; conclusions about that afternoon's odd visit with Jacob. The fear he felt, the nervous looking over the shoulder, and of course, leaving behind a 'just in case' letter.

She glanced down at Frank, then around him to the puddle of coagulating blood on the wooden floor. The coarse texture of the planks held little pools, showing no signs of drying up any time soon.

"Was it Crane?" She asked Frank.

"Get out of here miss, run!" Frank got up and shoved her to the door. He was petrified that Mr. Crane, who was still sitting in the booth, would kill her too.

"I still have something to do." She pulled Lynch Sullivan's revolver from her purse and pointed its heavy blue-black barrel at the darkened booth.

"Miss you don't want to do this!" Frank was pleading with her. He knew that if she went to pull the trigger, Mr. Crane would have only one option.

Her hands shook from all the excitement of the day. She would get a moment of rational thought and then would look down at the blood on her shoes and would whip the gun back up to firing position. Frank stood there, quietly and carefully, feeling hollow and artificial about how he and Jacob had spent that day.

She tried to ask Frank why he had done it, still pointing the gun at Crane as he watched her from the booth. She asked why it happened. Frank pointed at the shadowy seat.

A voice spoke from the booth; "I won't kill you. Just put down the gun." Frank squinted his eyes as he looked into the corner. After a minute or two he looked back at the corner and then went over to Mia. He slipped the revolver from her scared hands and told her to go home. "Please miss, go." She ran out the door and across the parking lot. The media crews were packing up their equipment, the crowds were thinned out. She ran for home, silently promising herself that it would be all right. She didn't believe it.

Back in the bar, the killer and Frank were looking at each other though Crane had the advantage of the shadow. "Why'd you kill that boy? He had nothing to do with that night." Frank expected an answer, but was confronted with a deep sigh. "Answer me!" The killer stretched his hand upward and turned a new lightbulb tightly into the dormant lamp. When the light came on, he found Jacob dressed in black, from neck to toe.

His old eyes grew large as he looked over the Armani suit, despising the streaks of blood on the lapel.

"Don't worry, I'll have it cleaned." Frank burst into happy tears. He laughed loudly and shook off the serious fear he had been feeling.

"Kid, what's happening?"

"It's just business as usual, right Frank?"

"You got it."

"Then how about a drink?"

"You got it kid."

"Frank?"

"Yeah kid?"

"The name's not kid. It's Mr. Crane, if you please."

Epilogue

Murder is wrong. No matter the motive, no matter the believed necessity, it is wrong. Too often, the ignorant and the brave are mixed in this act. Do not presume to know a man until you've lived his life. Do not believe you are infallible, that the matters from this novel could never happen to you. I made that mistake. I once lost a good friend to a situation similar to this novel, though there was no romance or poetry to his crime. If you do not believe in Mr. Crane, that is all the better for you, so that your dreams are filled with happy memories and life-long loves. As for me, it will prevent a dark visit from the black-suited gentleman who started his life on a farm in Minnesota. Take care not to be rude to tall gentlemanly strangers if you should choose to visit Arcadia. Merely nod your head or tip your hat in respect. Remember one thing for when you go on your nightly Arcadian walks: Nothing kills like rudeness.

About the Author

Anthony Blossingham's first published article appeared in the Traverse City Record-Eagle when he was 20 years old. After a number of published Feature Articles with the Record-Eagle, the Benzie County Record-Patriot, and numerous online publications, he began work on this novel.

A full-time student at Mott Community College in Flint MI, he has earned more credits through the Distance Learning Program than any other student in the history of that program. He hopes to finish his 4-year degree in the same independent study at one of Michigan's Universities.

He has inspired such emotion in his prior readers, showing a talent in making laughter and tears. Though his education is his main priority, he will be taking a hiatus during the summer months to travel and seek out inspiration for his next novel.

Printed in the United States
73224LV00003B/133